CHANNEL

Editors:
Cassia Gaden Gilmartin and Elizabeth Murtough

Irish Language Editor/ Eagarthóir Gaeilge and translator:
Aisling Ní Choibheanaigh Nic Eoin

Published with assistance from Publishing Intern S.R. Westvik.

Published in Dublin, Ireland by *Channel*.
Printed by City Print Limited.

Design and layout by Cassia Gaden Gilmartin.
Cover art by Isabel Nolan. Images provided by courtesy of the artist and Kerlin Gallery.
Cover design by Elizabeth Murtough.

Copyright *Channel* and individual contributors, 2023. All rights reserved. No part of this publication may be reproduced or transmitted without prior written permission from the publisher.

ISBN 978-1-9162245-9-9
ISSN 2712-0015

Connect with us: www.channelmag.org | info@channelmag.org
facebook.com/ChannelLiteraryMagazine/ | twitter: @Channel_LitMag | instagram: @channel_mag

Channel receives financial assistance from the Arts Council.
The position of Irish Language Editor/Eagarthóir Gaeilge is funded by Foras na Gaeilge.

Fiction

5	Podge Meehan	An Inconvenient Truth
23	Tremain Xenos	Fecundity
55	Tina Pisco	Ring of Fire
71	Roman Vai	Conversation Starters for Therapy
79	John Kaufmann	Genesis 6–9
96	Lucy Zhang	Reef Construction

Essay

39	Emilia Ong	Careful

Poetry

1	Thomas Mixon	No Trespassing
2	Beattie	Gnomes, Staring Up the Hill
3		A God Sits Watching the Ducks
18	Cliona O'Connell	In the Lord's Wood
20	Ayòdéjì Israel	Ten Couplets About My Body
21	Pádraig Ó Cuinneagáin	Deoir
36	Shakeema Edwards	New Mexico Whiptail Lizards
37		The Mating Behavior of Burying Beetles
38	Aoife Riach	New Year's Resolutions
48	Susanna Lang	Crow and Anti-Crow
50	Hui Ran	seeing the flood for the first time
51	Rose Malone	Tóraíocht: Scéal Ghráinne
53	Michael David Jewell	Camera Obscura

67	Joanne McCarthy	Garraíodóir
69	Lani O'Hanlon	A Café in Berlin
70		Landscape of the Body
76	Darren Higgins	The Floating Bridge
77	Diarmuid Cawley	Antiquity on a fault line
78		Ballyconnell, Sligo
90	Chinedu Gospel	If They Ask Me
92	Morgan Leathem Ventura	Aquatic Dirge
94	John Tinneny	Corpán
100	Yoni Hammer-Kossoy & Abby Yucht	Deconstructing Babels
106	Dáithí de Buitléir	Ráithín an Chloig, Bré
108	S.J. Delaney	Queer Pastoral
109		I Won't Stop Writing Queer Pastorals

Cover Art: *Dead talk (archaeologists)* and *Eurydice (dead again...) and Orpheus*, by Isabel Nolan

Isabel Nolan has an expansive practice that incorporates sculptures, paintings, textile works, photographs, writing and works on paper. Her subject matter is similarly comprehensive, taking in cosmological phenomena, religious reliquaries, Greco-Roman sculptures and literary/historical figures, examining the behaviour of humans and animals alike. These diverse artistic investigations are driven by intensive research, but the end result is always deeply personal and subjective. Exploring the "intimacy of materiality," Nolan's work ranges from the architectural – steel sculptures that frame or obstruct our path – to small handmade objects in clay, hand-tufted wool rugs illuminated with striking cosmic imagery, to drawings and paintings using humble gouache or colouring pencils. In concert, they feel equally enchanted by and afraid of the world around us, expressing humanity's fear of mortality and deep need for connection as well as its startling achievements in art and thought. Driven by "the calamity, the weirdness, horror, brevity and wonder of existing alongside billions of other preoccupied humans," her works give generous form to fundamental questions about the ways the chaos of the world is made beautiful or given meaning through human activity.

Isabel Nolan's solo exhibition *499 seconds* ran at Château La Coste, France, from 13 March to 4 June 2023. Previously, she has been the subject of solo exhibitions at Contemporary Art Gallery, Vancouver; Mercer Union, Toronto; London Mithraeum Bloomberg SPACE, London; Douglas Hyde Gallery, Dublin; IMMA, Dublin; Void Gallery, Derry; Kunstverein Graz, Austria; Kunstverein Langenhagen, Germany and Musée d'art moderne de Saint Etienne, France. Her work has also been exhibited at Palais de Tokyo, Paris; Salzburger Kunstverein; Centre of Contemporary Art, Geneva; Artspace, Sydney; Talbot Rice Gallery, Edinburgh; Scottish National Gallery, Edinburgh; Daejeon Museum of Art, South Korea and Beijing Art Museum of the Imperial City, Beijing. Nolan has participated in international group exhibitions and biennales including the Irish Pavilion at the Venice Biennale; Lofoten International Arts Festival (LIAF); Mediations Biennale, Poznan; Yugoslav Biennale of Young Artists, Vršac, Serbia; Glasgow International and EVA International Limerick.

We are grateful for Isabel's contribution of the following pieces to the cover of *Channel* Issue 9:

Front cover: *Dead talk (archaeologists)*, 2022
water-based oil on canvas
170 x 140 cm
66.9 x 55.1 in

Back cover: *Eurydice (dead again...) and Orpheus*, 2022
water-based oil on canvas
70 x 60 x 2 cm
27.6 x 23.6 x .8 in

Images provided by courtesy of the artist and Kerlin Gallery.

A note from Elizabeth Murtough

It's a Friday in October, the day that tips the week in the month that tips the year into the last pour of itself – the stream a little faster, slighter, readying our cups for the changeover rhythm of release and refill.

Publishing *Channel* biannually along this axis of seasonal change has trained my attention more acutely to the processorial nature of World. Like all things, *Channel* abides by the generation – fruition – fallow – seed cycle. This energy is embedded within the work itself – the felt and material cadences of making a literary magazine – and within the poems, stories and essays we receive.

Themes of potential, creation and the letting go of what was once-full thrum through each issue. In Issue 9, we repeatedly meet characters on the cusp – whether fleeing fire (Tina Pisco, p 55), facing rising waters (John Kaufmann, p 79), or navigating the grief of 'An Inconvenient Truth' (Podge Meehan, p 5), these stories speak to us of the ambiguities and hard realities of impermanence.

"Job, skill, or free time – this forest isn't mine," Thomas Mixon's speaker reminds us (p. 1). And yet, by stepping into the forest at all, "What a brutal, brilliant cyclone / you've already managed to stir" (Beattie, p 3). In centering the energy of change, these poems assure us it's the process, not its outcomes, that persists, "its ribs holding us within it" (Darren Higgins, p 76) "while the crows / [find] another tree" (Susanna Lang, p 49).

With the release of Issue 9, I, too, am off to find another tree "or whatever may be dwelling / in the silt, the clay, / the soil beneath our feet" (Morgan Leathem Ventura, p 92). It has been an immense privilege to edit *Channel* and to grow alongside this project for the last five years. What started as a way to connect with others has, from the start, facilitated deeper connection to myself, to my own individuation and creative energies. "I could line a face with my lessons," Hui Ran's speaker tells us (p 50), and I know the face of all my work to come will be coloured, lined, animated and made more open by my work with *Channel*.

My deepest thanks to the incredible writers who have trusted me with their work over the years; I have better learned and loved World through your words. I thank our readers, whose engagement with our work keeps the energy of exchange in motion; I thank our collaborators for joining us in the mad run of making; I thank Cassia, whose partnership has made that making possible; and I thank my community, whose enduring love and relation I trust "as a source / of (say it!) / salvation / from a centre / we can never know" (Cliona O'Connell, p 19).

Finally, I thank *Channel* itself, for all it has given me and for the grace now to say goodbye, "leaving a trace just like I learned I shouldn't" (Mixon, p 1).

A note from Cassia Gaden Gilmartin

In her beautiful poem 'The Mating Behaviour of Burying Beetles,' Shakeema Edwards writes of how the corpse of a blackbird is given new life: two carrion beetles dig a grave for the bird and embalm it with spit, preparing it as food for their young so that, "when their tenerals emerge in June, / it feels the air under their hindwings" (p.37). There's an intimacy to this process of digestion and assimilation, described with a tenderness that honours such blending of subjectivities.

In today's climate of overwhelming hostility, with fatal tensions playing out within homes and on the international stage, the existence of such symbiosis strikes me as a fragile miracle. So, too, does the opportunity we at *Channel* have been granted to publish poems like Shakeema's. Publishing is itself a collaborative process, one that often blurs the lines between the work of author, publisher and reader and that calls for a great deal of trust. For a writer, to publish is to pull words out from the most vulnerable reaches of the psyche into the open, leaving them "mortifyingly exposed" (Emilia Ong, p.47). It's also to court the kinds of change that can come over a work when it's exposed to editorial intervention, book design, a marketing strategy, and placement within a context of other people's words. A poem, as it becomes part of a publication, takes on new meanings. As editors, we may choose to approach our work with caution – to edit and package work with respect for the unknowable depths of other minds, with our ears and hearts open to feedback, and to hope that through these efforts our role will feel more like support and less like violence – but the effects we may have on a piece, and on its creator, are multifaceted, and often discoverable only in the throes of collaboration.

For me, one of the great joys of publishing is that, just as our platform reshapes the words our contributors share with us, it is shaped by them. *Channel* is constituted, and continually reconstituted, from the input of our writers, our editorial team, our cover artists, all those readers and contributors who offer us chances to reflect on our work, and those who reflect their sense of what we do back at us. This commingling of voices is rarely straightforward, and always holds the potential for injury – as Abby Yucht puts it, "We come together and we collapse, like a burst eardrum" (p.105). The attention demanded by our collaborators' work, and the often-inarticulable resonances through which their ideas come alive in us, can be all-consuming: in the words of Yoni Hammer-Kossoy, "Their songs invade my sleep until my sleep / becomes song" (p.103). The result, when our work together goes well, is not a simple bringing together of separate pieces but a transmutation into something new, ever-changing but irreducibly itself.

With this issue, we say goodbye to half of the four-person publishing team who have given life to this year's *Channel*. Our 2023 Publishing Intern, S.R. Westvik, will finish their time with us, and our co-founding editor, Elizabeth Murtough, will step away after five years' work to give attention to other projects. When I asked Lizzi, back in 2019, to create *Channel* with me, I did it in part because I already loved her work as a poet – because I wanted the journal we might publish to be coloured by her poetry. It has been, but *Channel* has also been shaped by Lizzi and S.R. in ways that I couldn't have predicted, and in ways that I may never fully understand. The ideas that form and find their way to these pages in the coming years will not be their responsibility, but will, in an important sense, belong to us all.

Channel's 2022 Publishing Intern, Dorje de Burgh, wrote in an editorial note for Issue 7, at the end of his work with us, of the transformative potential to be found in "local, small-scale community building centred around writing, reading and the sharing of art and knowledge. Making things. Making things together."

Thank you, Lizzi and S.R., for the energy you've given to our community. May we all continue making things, apart and together.

A note from our 2023 Publishing Intern, S.R. Westvik

As I write this, Storm Ciarán is looming over these islands and set to bring a deluge of water and whistling winds. Coming on the heels of Samhain, as one part of the year turns into the other, I can't help but feel a sense of quiet reckoning. It coincides with the end of my ten months at *Channel* and the departure of Elizabeth, but also the launch of a new issue and the flourishing of our Irish language work stewarded by Aisling. I feel a deep resonance with the work in this issue, observing the regularity of the turning year and increasing irregularity of meteorological phenomena. So much of the ideas and imagery within these pages speak as much to that which is static—the things of nature—as to that which is not—the nature of things. It feels, to me, to be an apt issue to close out my time at *Channel*.

Cassia and Elizabeth have already spoken to the incisive, immersive works of poetry and prose bookended by the spellbinding paintings of Isabel Nolan. I would like to therefore spend a few words reflecting on how important the existence of *Channel* itself is, as an agent of community building as well as artistic growth.

Working for *Channel* has been a revelation as to how publishing could be—especially when it comes to engaging with nature and the crucial ways we interact with it. I came to *Channel* from a varied background, steeped in a literary upbringing but with a current focus on war trauma, and an interest in its intersection with the fantastical. The beauty of the space this magazine provides is that it actively welcomes and uplifts new, distinct, individual ways to approach our common ecosphere and our common crises, and therein find solidarity. Some of my fondest memories of my time here will be the deep sense of community I have felt at every stage of the journey. Be it answering messages from longtime readers, welcoming returning contributors, or meeting new writers at our intimate (yet very vibrant) launches and mingling with the guests, I have felt an almost mycellic sense of connection with each and every individual that has been part of making nine iterations of a wonderful whole—with many more to come.

It has been an honour and a privilege to work with and learn from Cassia and Elizabeth, whose erudition and work ethic are aspirational, and to work alongside Aisling, whose sensitivity and skill with language inspires me. I wish Elizabeth all the best as she takes the next step in her artistic journey, and wish so much luck to Cassia and Aisling moving forward with *Channel*. And to the writers and readers—it has been one of the most treasured experiences of my life to have been a part of bringing these works to publication.

Thomas Mixon

No Trespassing

I love the stupid crows and wasps that bother me
on walks. This is why I squawk at the empty truck
next to the No Trespassing sign. A man is somewhere
out here with me, and I don't care about his hobby,
job, skill, or free time – this forest isn't mine,
but neither is it his. I love dorsal recumbencies
in snakes, in turkeys, in animals I cannot see
right next to me – previously lying down, startled
at my primal howl. I had meant to let them be,
but since there is another person through the leaves,
it may as well be me that breaks their peace,
a softie who would rather interrupt their nap
or play, than hear them shot, pesticide-sprayed.
I love the flies, the deer chock-full of ticks,
the over-eager squirrel guarding hemlocks
that nuthatches would love to call their home.
If I was alone, I'd shut my mouth, and never write
this poem. But since I'm not, I tilt my head
backwards and scream just like the fisher cats
that displace my dreams – the breakfast crumbs
escaping off my sleeves, generating trails,
disrupting the ecology of marsh and streams,
leaving a trace just like I learned I shouldn't.

Beattie

Gnomes, Staring Up the Hill

The cracks in the gnomes' cheeks
let their grunts pour over the fence, up the hill.
They plead with the slopes no matter how

we turn them, how we rotate their feet
and point them at the house, the patio.

The neighbours smashed theirs to crockery
when the turning stopped
their children sleeping.

They have been caught smuggling parcels
over back walls, packages we can't

prise open. The neighbour asks
if we've thought of nails,

if we'd crack
their red boots open

wide as an eyehole, to pin them
into place.

We watched a friend try and the screams
cut the night air into couch grass
all the way to the morning.

We tell them we will manage it.

Beattie

A Gods Sits Watching the Ducks

A squall, roaring where my
lungs meet. I'm sure nobody
has been so beautiful
as you, watching the ducks.
What a brutal, brilliant cyclone
you've managed already to stir, at your barely
audible age, zipping through
the corridors of my chest and of my heart.
You are the wind god, surely – this adorable
maelstrom, giggling in the depths of me –

this is all I can encounter, this
overwhelms whenever I am
near you, though I will
admit it is harder at certain moments, such as just now,
when you insisted you were also the god
of the waters and needed to be right amongst
your people, the pondweed and the minute fish, though I,
having gone down to the biggest water
every day and communed with the true
god of salt and wetness, know
that you cannot swim and will drown
if allowed to go chasing swans around,
after first being bitten – I could not
sit and bear to watch that, see you bitten
by somebody else, some stranger, some
monster with a song like steam
emptying from an industrial coffee machine.

But we have forgotten
such outbursts now. We have moved
on and have settled down into sitting
calmly on a bench and watching
the water and its birds from a distance.

Podge Meehan

An Inconvenient Truth

Dad died weeks before the wedding, which he would have smirkingly described with his sideways nod as "inconvenient." He went for his usual walk, around the block just before sunset, fiddling with his new bluetooth headphones and listening to these podcasts about murders in rural Ireland that for some reason he couldn't get enough of. The path he tread unchanging, he would make it down the gentle slope to the back of the next estate, the newer one where the semi-detached, slightly more middle class folk looked back up at us in disdain, where he had found a wall to sit facing west to watch the sun disappear into the low distant hills. The mother would stay at home and get some scones that she had made in batches out of the freezer, and she'd get the tea on and wait for him to come back, only that time he didn't come back. They said it was a stroke, a sudden calamity of the brain, and he slumped forwards off the wall and it took us ages to find him. Maybe if he'd been at home the mother could have called an ambulance and because the house, where they had spent their whole married lives together and where I and my brother had grown up, was close to the hospital, maybe, just maybe, something could have been done to save him, even if that meant he was a vegetable of sorts, which again is something he would have smirkingly described as inconvenient.

Don't mind me, he would say. I don't want to be in the way now.

We buried him, a huge inconvenient funeral, a parading of dull ageing acquaintances from a life lived medium-well, and that was that. Only of course it wasn't. Everything was changed, forever tainted with the reverberations of the moment his brain thirsted for the calm flow of blood and the oxygen carted within. Life went on, the days just kept coming whether you were ready for them or not, decisions had to be made that no one wanted to make and we, the three left behind, bickered and bit and talked shit about each other on WhatsApp.

The wedding was delayed, first by a year and then, because the biological clock was ticking, by two years. At least that's how we presented it, but realistically we got pissed on pink sangria in Madrid visiting some college friend of his with a new husband, and if it hadn't been for the fact that I was going to marry him anyway I would have had the abortion I had always feared. So by the time the wedding came round it felt like a normal Saturday with too much shit to do. A mighty inconvenience. The baby was still breastfeeding and the dress had been mangled by the Eastern European girls in the tailors, not unlike how my body had been mangled by the baby, and I was too afraid of being racist to complain, and anyway I had a broken fingernail which caught and pulled threads on it and made it even worse, and the mother couldn't turn herself off and pointed out every loose thread before moving on to everything that was wrong with everything including saying you should have picked a sunnier day for it the photos will be dull. I didn't feel at all like a girl becoming a woman, which, despite my better judgement, was how I had imagined it would feel, but like a woman in full flight, the magic completely drained. There was no sublime adulthood to which I would graduate and beam with the joy of well-handled responsibility, there was just more of the same, frustrated instead with the inconvenience of an undefinable duty. I just breathed deep and used the strategies the grief counsellor had taught me. Switch off the mother. Talk to Dad in your mind. And that got me through it. That and Colin. He's solid. Thank fuck.

I didn't even have a drink. I only pretended to sup at the champagne and then glibly abandoned the glass high on a bookshelf in the front room of the posh hotel that were none too happy about the fact we had cancelled the wedding in the first place and through a series of very formal emails tried to get us to pay a second deposit. The photos were exhausting, the day was clammy and cold and the mother complained of her arthritis so much my own fingers ached. By the time we got to the speeches I was ready to get into my pyjamas, curl up with Colin, turn on a slow burner of a film that we could talk over and just say thank fuck that's all over now let's focus on the rest of our lives, which have already been happening all this time.

It was supposed to have been a surprise. I don't know why they thought, the two of them, that it was a good idea. The mother had found on Dad's laptop a file titled "An Inconvenient Truth," a nod to the academic life of

Environmental Science he had helped me negotiate a path to. The file was ostensibly a rough draft of the speech he would make after walking me up the aisle and happily handing me over to Colin. I had baulked at the idea of one man giving me away to another man, the feminism I had learned from books finally getting enough traction in general culture that I could actually say so, but Dad had seemed crestfallen by the suggestion he wouldn't get to do it, so we came to the compromise that Colin's mother, god bless her she wouldn't know which side of the bread to butter, would walk him up the aisle first so it was more of a generational thing, parents handing their children over to the idea of marriage, which is what we had signed up for. And because that was the idea we had settled on I had no argument against the mother when she said she would walk me up the aisle in Dad's absence, which for fuck sake couldn't the woman just let me have one thing without her.

The surprise was the speech. I didn't know anything about it. Delivered by Tommy, my brother, doing his not-as-accurate-as-he-thinks impression of Dad. So there you have your brother half cut, he's not really managed adulthood so well, reading words your dead Dad wrote, saying things like Sparkle of Joy and Depths of Love and conjuring memories Dad had treasured of me to illustrate the independence I courted without compromise and the sting of pure love he felt for me, and with every cunt you've ever known in your life sitting around stuffed full of overpriced steak looking at you and three professional photographers to capture the moment. Jesus they can all fuck off.

To be fair, Tommy realised half way through that he'd fucked up and that it was a terrible idea. His plus one, a different brunette from the one invited to the original wedding, looked memeable as a Get Me Out Of Here smile set like concrete on her face. Tommy stumbled over some words as the realisation hit him. As a teacher you know when someone with no experience of public speaking starts to shit the bed, and he nervously brushed past some stuff I haven't been able to go back and read, and he landed instead at the last paragraph, the inconvenient truth.

There is, he said, finding his voice again, relishing the fact that the words were powerful and he'd get to go off and smash whiskeys in a minute. There is an inconvenient truth. You are everything we could have wanted you to become. You are strong and willful and caring. You are funny and smart and adventurous. You are able to read to the centre of people and you are impossible to fool. And the inconvenient truth that is sitting here staring us all in the face is that you do not need us anymore. You are complete. Today I lose my little girl as she launches herself fully prepared into the future she has clearly mapped for herself. We love you as much as you will love your own children. The wheel of life once again reaches the apex. Goodbye child. It was an immense pleasure to have been your father.

    I mean what the fuck do you do in that situation? Do you run off to the bathrooms? Do you just wail like a hungry infant? Do you just say thanks through gritted teeth and wait desperately for the moment to move on? And then the cunt just hands me the microphone and I just couldn't and I managed a weak I'm sorry and broke down sobbing and Colin grabbed the microphone but couldn't find the switch to turn if off off so the whole place is getting me at a thousand decibels weeping for the loss of my father. You try having a dance after that.

You should have thanked the people for coming, the mother said to me later on as the party was entering the ember stage. The fight in me slumped and cowered and backed away and I sighed yeah Mam, too late now though. And she went on about the thank you cards I would have to write, and the local stationery shop just down from the shopping centre they have some lovely ones and the girl in there is really nice and she's in a support group for something because I've seen her down the church after mass on a Wednesday so she could do with some cheering up.

    Thanks Mam.

    You know, she said then, grabbing my elbow, when I got married I was much younger than you. My own mother your grandmother waited until the car had come to take us away because that's what you did in those days you left your own wedding and you'd get a clap and all that we went on to Dublin to the airport to catch a flight that was the first time I was on an airplane going on my honeymoon with your dad and it was very strange because doing something that grown up was very sudden for me and she grabbed my arm like this and she said into my ear No matter what happens, always be prepared. Put some money away. Because if you ever need to run away, you run and don't let money stop you.

Thanks Mam, but I don't think things are quite the same these days, I said, I can always divorce him.

I looked across to Colin, helping his cousin's youngest try on his suit jacket and laughing heartily with a pint held high and straight in his other hand and I could not imagine life without the ease he made me feel.

You listen to me love, my mother said, her grasp slipping into a drunken pinch, it's not just about having that money just in case. It's about knowing you have that money just in case. You won't feel stuck if you know how to get out, and sometimes knowing you can is enough to get you through.

I looked at my mother and I didn't recognise the face on her, layered with make-up and rounded off with an earnest determined frown. Keeping her at arms length since adolescence had been hard work, trying to minimise the psychological rockiness she would set in motion meant communication between us had been distilled into something not quite what either of us thought. I imagined her for the first time as an unhappily married woman, which was a new idea because my father was the more easygoing, more gentle and respectful of the two. I had always attributed her unhappiness to her, a floating separate thing that unfolded and tried to touch you but for which ultimately she was the source. Maybe it was the emotion of the day fraying my ragged sense of self but she suddenly felt like a mother to me, with a desperate kind of love that I had misread all this time, and I hugged her and that took her by surprise. She didn't hug back but sort of placed her arm across my back, waiting for the moment to pass. Then she walked off to retie Tommy's tie and to firmly give out to him for drunkenly photobombing family friends.

Life went on. The honeymoon lasted three days in West Cork where it rained mistily non-stop. We cut it short using the excuse of my motherly hormones, oh how I missed the baby, but really because sitting in a pub on the edge of the world and drinking peach juice was not a good use of our time. I regretted naming the baby after Dad and so referred to him as baby and visibly tightened whenever anyone used the real name. Tommy got a job in America and left with a suitcase of inherited ill-fitting suits. He left the brunette and the mother behind but they still went to mass together on Wednesdays and helped out with the St. Vincent de Paul deliveries on Saturdays. I started liking the brunette but also felt sorry she wasn't enough of a person for me to bother to remember her name. Colin started asking questions about a second child and I felt like I was on pause, watching from a distance as everyone else somehow managed.

You are not going to turn into your mother, Colin said. It was a recurrent topic of conversation now. I looked at the baby and the love I had thought would flow through me and lift me up and carry me through life was not forthcoming. The thing my dad had described that had brought him so much joy was not in me. Instead I was like my mother. Waiting for my turn.

I discussed the mother's secret money with Colin.

Makes sense for that time, he said, they couldn't get divorced, no one was on their side.

How would you feel if I did that?

You do what you need to do, he said. It's your money. Feed and clothe the kid and you won't hear me complain after that.

Do you think she wanted to?

I'd run away from her.

I went back to work after maternity leave plus sabbatical plus Dr. Kelvin gave me three months for mental health reasons and I threw myself into it. The summer came along and the students went home and the research centre packed full of dry-skinned pony-tailed suburban nerds on internships and an International Fund for Human Health Development in conjunction with the European Union offered us ridiculous money to work on how to package carbon offsetting so big businesses could invest in the future and the roundtable meetings were pulsating with so many ideas that just didn't square but the University was against any kind of attitude which wasn't total deference, there was too much money riding on the venture.

I'm a scientist, not a marketing schrench, I almost screamed at Dr. Kelvin in his big boss chair.

Maybe you came back too soon, he said. We'll keep the job open for you.

Did you write the thank you cards yet? The mother asked day one of my I'm depressed and maybe I've fucked my professional career leave.

She sat at the kitchen table judging the mess of baby paraphernalia, unfolded clothes and toast crumbs.

I won't have tea now, she says, you're too busy.
Make it yourself Mam.
I don't want to be in the way.
She'd come round to ask me to go with her.
You need a break from all this love.
She admitted she still had the money. Enough to pay for a hotel and then a boat to England and I'd stay upstairs in some terraced house in Coventry, she said, I knew a girl from there, and I'd have enough until I could get work. Sometimes I worried if I had enough to bring you and your brother along, who'd look after ye when I was off working to pay the bills. Maybe I'd have to leave ye behind.
You make it sound as if you were an abused spouse Mam.
My own mother would have run if the lord hadn't intervened and taken your grandfather away.
I'm happy with Colin.
Happy is not what I'd say.
He's not what the problem is.
Will I make scones?

She paid for everything. She must have had over ten grand in the account, scurried away like a paranoid squirrel. She rang a travel agent they'd used to go on a seniors trip to Lanzarote, the last trip together. She'd complained about the whole thing. The other members of the group were old and infirm and the food was too Spanish; fish with their heads still on them. This time they'll know what I want, she said. She asked for the most expensive hotel in the west, which I'm sure had the agent's eyes ringing like a cartoon cash register. Colin was supportive. His mam and sister-in-law Marie would be around to help.

We had to take the bus to Galway because she had sold the car after Dad died as she didn't like driving and I had to leave our car for Colin to get to work. The bus arrived late and the driver got off to smoke and she asked him if he were Irish and he said no and she sat in the front seat behind him. She was quiet the whole trip concentrating on not succumbing to travel sickness. In Galway we had to walk a few blocks to the other bus station, the one for the private buses, past vibrant bars and a hot dog stand. She went into the Centra on the corner and came out with a hairbrush and a tabloid newspaper.

I like to read the sports, she said. And tell your father how his teams are getting on.

We got on the bus to Clifden and the mother asked the driver if he could drop us off at the hotel and he said that wasn't a stop and the best he could do was at the turnoff where we'd have about a mile to go. She asked him where he was from and he said Lodz with careful Anglicised sounds and she didn't know where that was but didn't ask. I called the hotel and they said they'd send a car to get us.

Once the bus hit Connemara the mist settled in and it was just like West Cork again. A blanket of thick snotty dullness layered over the sharp sheeeeesh roll of the bus. Then it started to rain, big infrequent drops dying against the side windows like spattered insects. As we neared the foothills of sudden stone mountains, the bus heaved slightly to the side of the road. There was no hard shoulder or road markings of any kind, only a green ditch starting to pool with mud.

Madam, the bus driver said, the hotel is up that road.

But where is the car from the hotel to pick us up?

No one responded. The atmosphere in the bus tightened. Legs were crossed, squeezed tighter, headphones tinkered with, heads began to turn to stare in other directions.

You can't just abandon us at the side of the road. It's raining.

Come on Mam, I said, hurrying down the steps. I dragged our suitcases out of the luggage compartment, having to move heavy backpacks unhelpfully stacked in front of them. I dragged one through a puddle in frustration, keeping my calm while the mother argued.

Reluctantly, and loudly complaining that he was abandoning an old lady at the side of the road in the rain, the mother came down the steps, took my hand and turned to glare through the closing door at the driver and then, as the bus pulled away, at the other passengers who all chose to look straight ahead, afraid to meet her stare.

The minibus had to pick up some Americans, they'll be along shortly, I said.

We stood in the rain, no umbrellas. There were mountains behind us and we turned to watch them trying to wrest themselves free of the clouds. There was a river at the side of the road in the ditch and a duck made noises but I could not see it.

Your father would have driven, she said and started walking up the road. Failing to call her back I dragged the suitcases along the uneven surface and followed. As we walked, the mountain won the struggle against the clouds, the rain blew into the distance where it was still clearly visible like heavy grey pencil strokes from the sky. A rainbow appeared which neither of us mentioned and my phone rang. It was the minibus driver asking where we had got to and after explaining a moment later he appeared behind us, pulling into the side of the road by the ditch, helping us with our bags and listening intently to the mother.

You should say sorry for leaving an old lady to fend for herself in this wilderness, she said.

Yes ma'am, he said, sorry.

Where are you from? She asked.

Wuuch, he said.

She refused his hand to climb into the minibus and was visibly startled to find the minibus almost full of well-dressed, round-faced, inconspicuous Americans, six in all. She mumbled greetings and, embarrassed, sat herself into one of the remarkably comfortable leather seats and crossed her arms, perhaps trying not to cry. I climbed into the front seat and said a bright hello to the crowd which was welcomed by all and I pointed to the rainbow and cameras and phones were produced and everyone leaned to the west side of the vehicle to snap for the folks back home.

I waited until she was in the shower before I rang Colin.
　She's a nightmare. If she'd run away back in the day I don't think anyone would have missed her. She keeps asking the Polish lads where they're from like she's trying to make a point. She thinks the world owes her a favour.
　The baby is fine, he said. He's asleep on Marie's shoulder. I think she wants one for herself. Maybe he'll have cousins soon enough.
　I could hear Marie laughing saying Stop that now in the background.
　We said our I love yous and I got ready for dinner.

In the bar after the tiny-portion many-course meal we ordered a local beer that was deeply bitter and sat next to the fireplace in huge leather armchairs. Everything was the colour of wood, including the beer. I felt on the cusp of relaxing but unable to release myself into it.
　I don't know why posh people like eating foam so much, she was saying.
　I was exhausted.
　The Americans came into the bar, wowed by the extravagance of the antiques and the solidity of the architecture.
　We're really in the past now, one of them said.
　I tried to catch the mother's eye to share a derisive look but she was intently watching them.
　They sat too close to us, applying campfire rules to the indoors. The mother immediately sat straighter and spoke brighter, obviously trying to defuse the first impression she had made earlier.
　My son has just moved to America, she said.
　Oh wow, one of them said, that's nice. Is he happy?
　He's happy on the phone, but you know children, they're terrified of telling you they're not happy in case you try to rescue them.
　The Americans all laughed.
　I shirked further into the armchair, the heat of the fire and the

lightheadedness of the beer agitating me. There were four of them, all now staring at my mother. The small talk was now big talk. The oldest of the group, a man in his late sixties who had half of one ear completely missing, took the lead.

Whereabouts does he live? He asked.

Maybe we can check up on him, another added.

Someplace near Boston. Summer town or something like that.

Oh Boston is lovely, my first cousins live there, let me ring them.

Maybe they know him, the mother said.

Don't be stupid, I said, and the silence that followed vibrated with tension for a long moment and when the conversation continued I suddenly felt excluded from it. Like they'd turned their backs on me with their eyes and timbre.

When they discovered the company Tommy worked for, the old lady rang her cousins because their neighbour worked high up in that company, he was well-known to the family, they'd all been at a graduation together, and they were given his number and he checked the company database and there indeed was the file for Tommy, isn't he handsome, and will I recommend him for a promotion? Oh that would be lovely indeed. Have a nice day.

Back in the room the mother told me off.

All you have to do is ask, she said. Be happy for your brother.

Afterwards I couldn't sleep. The mother looked frail in the moonlight coming through the enormous bay window, wrapped up in her dreams and heavy duty duvet with its richly embroidered cotton cover. I sat in the little alcove with the window open a crack and tried not to think, which is always harder for the trying. I waited for birdsong but the exhaustion got to me first and I fell asleep where I was.

Is that how you sleep at home? She asked me.

Yes mam. I sleep on the floor by the window, I said sarcastically.

Well, I don't know, she said, what goes on in your marriage.

We had the breakfast. Probably the most expensive tea and toast I'll ever have. The minibus dropped us down the road beside a lake and next to the start of the hiking track up the stone mountain.

The twelve pins they're called, the driver said. You can hike all twelve in the one day but you'll need the best shoes.

We're only going for a look, the mother said. Keep your phone on.

The path curled through the grounds of a youth hostel and some young, healthy-looking Europeans sat at a wooden picnic table watching us pass by in our brand new matching tracksuits. I gave a gentle wave and a smile and only one of them waved back.

I bet their tea and toast wasn't twenty quid, I said.

You're always complaining, she said.

The ground was wet and boggy in patches and completely impassable in places where the wheels of a tractor had created divots big enough to form pools, causing us to walk through the spongy deep grasses littered with sheep shit. The gradient was winding and soft at first but after a few minutes became sharp and jaunty, and the mother stopped to consider her options each time the path surged upwards.

Fat shapeless clouds hurried across the sky, plunging us into shadow, and each time they passed the sun burst joyfully from the sky again and this dramatic racing of shadows reflecting the turbulence above felt both liberating and insignificant. Behind us the land stretched further and further into the distance. The land seeped into a lake and the lake was peppered with a thousand tiny islands and the lake and the sky and the islands fused together to make a jagged horizon that made the ground under your feet seem unstable and the sensation was exhilarating.

The mother stopped to rest, sitting on a damp mossy stone, and she stood again when the young Europeans from the youth hostel sauntered by in single file, not more than a nod of greeting from the bunch. They were loudly talking in their own language, maybe Dutch, maybe some Scandinavian tongue, maybe even something more Eastern, but the tone was happy and full of breath.

They're scaring all the rabbits away, the mother said.

The clouds were coming in faster and fatter and the threat of rain could be seen in the colours of the jagged horizon. I followed the Europeans. They were already dots in the distance, moving fast and climbing shortcuts they couldn't resist to link the corners of the zigzag path. I walked. My heart started to race. The mother called.

Come back! Where are you going? I've had enough.

And when she saw I wasn't stopping.

Hey. Hey. Hey! Come back here or that.

And when I still wouldn't stop, my phone rang and it was her and I put the phone on a wet rock and let it sing its forlorn tune.

I walked.

The rain started behind me. I did not turn to look at it. The distance disappeared. The Europeans no longer visible in the mist. I walked. The path became soggy and my footsteps slurped at the ground and I turned and could not see the mother below nor the lake with the islands behind or anything but an all enveloping mist and I walked. I walked until my feet burned with wetness and effort, until I could feel the heaviness of the water on my tracksuit, until I could hear the young friends in the distance, shouting about the rain or the visibility. I walked until I reached the top and to the south the sun was shining again and slowly the light spread like spilling water and from left to right the land appeared below and beyond me, revealing the lake and the islands and I wiped the wetness from my face and saw what we had come to see, the stretching of everything into nothing and my mother a faint dot in the distance that cannot be wiped away.

Cliona O'Connell

In the Lord's Wood

after Mary Oliver

Look, the light
is turning
the tree's body
into a pillar
of shadow,
is shaking
the slight
metallic bright
like salt
on the fallen
cinnamon leaves
and on the bare
roots draped
over the grey
sloped shoulders
of the narrow stream
that disappears
for months at a time
for years
everything
I have ever learned
in my lifetime
leads back to this: the cold,
the mast and the must of loss,
the damp landscape
whose lit lines rise

as a source
of (say it!)
salvation
from a centre
we can never know

To believe in this life
it helps
to do three things:
to know seeing
as the latewood
of loving;
to welcome shadow
and leaf
as familiar
strangers patterning
the heart's path
and when
you have lost
yourself in the heft
of your left leaves
to remember
how to walk
back to the world

Ayòdéjì Israel
Ten Couplets About My Body

i hold my body in fragments
and hope i do not break away.

i snatch a strain from God's moustache
and paste it on my skin. i will live forever.

i throw my flesh against the heavens
and hope it carries a butter of God's grace.

i hide my body from my country and become
a star. i will shine even if my country does not.

i become wind and scatter like breeze.
i want to see the world beyond myself.

i pour my blood inside a bird flying into the sky.
the blood is a sample of the wars i survived.

i renounce the brevity of this world. my
body will stay alive like the breath of life.

i remember the psalm of my father: i will
be whiter than snow; than cassava pulp.

i pour my spirit into the mouth of God. he
will swallow my sin and pass me out alive.

i say this with the remaining breath in my nostrils:
i kiss the lips of the Almighty and swallow his spit.

Pádraig Ó Cuinneagáin

Deoir

Triailim ar an tobar arís. Piseog fanta ó m'óige.
Idir chaonach agus chloch a luíonn sé sa talamh.
Anuas ar mo ghlúna ar an ithir thais.

Dearcaim san uisce dorcha broghach.
Faoi mar a thumann mo shúile níos doimhne sa dorchadas,
Chun tosaigh tagann fear.

Fear freagraí.

        Ólaim deoir.

                Tuigim céard atá fúm.

Pádraig Ó Cuinneagáin

Tear

I go to the well again. A remembered superstition from my youth.
Between moss and stone, it lies in the ground.
Down on my knees on the damp earth.

I look into that dark, murky water.
As my eyes dive deeper in the darkness,
a man appears

A man of answers.

        I drink a tear.

            I understand what to do.

Tremain Xenos

Fecundity

Just before Golden Week, Uncle Shigenori drove his *kei*-truck into a wall and woke up in hospital with no idea what happened. Grandma Kimie called my wife to go and reason with him: he'd been lashing out at the doctors and nurses, insisting on going home. My wife returned from Central Hospital with the announcement that she'd persuaded him to remain there till they could be sure he didn't have a concussion. The real problem, she said, was that he couldn't eat hospital food. He couldn't chew. That's why he'd been living on beer for days on end.

"He's just over sixty," my wife said. "But his body is over eighty."

Grandma Kimie is over eighty. For a long time I thought the two of them were husband and wife. My wife refers to them collectively as "Togawa"—after the area where they live—a name I could never remember.

"Your uncle and his wife?" I once asked her.

"That's his mother," she laughed. "Well—not his biological mother."

My wife refers to her relatives by name or location more often than by relationship. She calls her maternal grandfather Hirō-san. I know him only through faded sepia photographs in the crusty albums on the shelves of our library. He took his wife's surname and moved into her family house with her six unwed sisters, of whom only Kimie and Kiyoko are still alive. My wife's maternal grandmother died not long after birthing her two children, Shigenori and Setsuko. Hirō then married his widow's youngest sister, Kimie, though no children were born between them. Setsuko moved away on marriage and had two children of her own: Anna, my wife, and her sister, Emi.

Grandma Kimie and Uncle Shigenori never left the house in Togawa.

On a visit to Grandma Kiyoko in the care home, I heard she'd once asked Uncle Shigenori if he'd ever had or wanted a girlfriend. He was so angry he refused to talk to her for the rest of the day.

"That kid," Grandma Kiyoko said, "Has never known a woman."

Grandma Kiyoko's late husband had been a high-ranking bureaucrat. It was her inherited largesse that provided the down payment on our house. Planning for children, Anna and I bought a two-storey *kominka* with three extra bedrooms. Seven childless years later, we wish we'd gone in for less house and more land.

For the former owners, our garden had been nothing more than a convenient disposal site for broken roof tiles, tin cans, and boulders. Much of the plot was more impacted gravel and trash than soil. Year by year we dug up the debris, replacing it each spring with compost. We grew tomatoes, zucchini, kabocha squash, capsicums, artichokes, and kale. From grafts, we planted fig trees and citrus: lemon, yuzu, and *ponkan*. Along the perimeter we planted scores of rose bushes, which now hold up our crumbling bamboo fence rather than take support from it. In the daylight hours, walkers in their billed caps and plaid shirts and utility trousers stopped to lean over the roses and ask how on earth we used those exotic vegetables.

Although the climate would allow planting in early April, my teaching schedule left me no time to prepare the garden before the Golden Week holidays—and until then, Uncle Shigenori was always busy ploughing for neighbouring farmers in Togawa. But since his machine can do in an hour what takes me three days by hand, for the past few years it's made sense to wait for him.

From the stairwell, I heard my wife on the telephone with Grandma Kimie.

"He needs his eyedrops." In the pause my memory replays Grandma Kimie's caw of *Hennh?* "Eyedrops." Pause. "*Drops* for his *eyes.*" Pause. "*Medicine* he puts in his *eyes. EYE … DROPS.*"

I stepped onto the porch to survey our scraggly jungle of sorrel, horsetail, purslane, and crabgrass.

"Uncle Shigenori will be in hospital for the rest of the week," came my wife's voice behind me. "He's in no shape for gardening."

I steeled myself against sweat and blisters, and went to the shed for tools.

After seven years, the hoe went in easily. It hit no obstacles but stones. I swung. Stepped backward. Swung again. The soil loosened. I churned up long rows from the fence to the garden path. It would take me three days if I finished each day before sunset.

My wife emerged now and then to push her denim hat over her eyes, drape a towel over her shoulders, and gather the rows into long straight mounds perpendicular to the garden path. An ultrasonic device hooked to her belt loop kept the mosquitoes from devouring her: once bitten, her welts wouldn't heal for days. She squatted, crumbled the dirt between her gloved hands and cast aside the broken glass. Sweat sparkled on flesh banded with decades-old scars the sun can never tan.

"How deep were the cuts?" I asked.

"All the way to the muscle fibres. The taxi driver was horrified."

"Why'd you call a taxi?"

"I couldn't drive." Laughing, she recalled reaching the hospital in the middle of the night, when the only doctor available to sew the wounds was her psychiatrist. He'd never done stitches on lacerations so deep. His hands trembled. A dozen nurses gathered to watch the operation.

Then Anna straightened, smiled, and waved at the old woman next door, whose cockerel always rouses us at dawn. Behind her lumbered her middle-aged son, unable to work, impervious to greetings. Anna wiped her face with her towel and watched them disappear along the road.

"I wonder who'll take care of him when his mother dies," she said. Then she reminded me to be inside before sundown—and made me promise that, if I wasn't, I wouldn't look at the road.

Ours is a sparsely populated but absurdly large municipality, having absorbed legions of villages and hamlets since its inception. Reaching Togawa takes a half hour drive through a thinning townscape, where the buildings are more often factories or warehouses than shops, the staggered residences increasingly larger and more poorly tended. Tract after tract of glistening chartreuse paddies, and hills quilted with deep kudzu stretching its aimless bent tendrils over retaining walls and guardrails. Togawa lies just beyond the prefectural prison, along a winding highway through cedar-covered mountains where locals stare out disdainfully from houses of rust held down by discarded tyres. Grandma Kimie and Uncle Shigenori live across a bridge from the main road, on the only strip of flat land between a sheer wooded hillside and a wide, shallow creek that runs through bushes of mugwort. Once, on our way to visit them with Grandma Kiyoko, my wife pointed out the route her mother and uncle used to walk to school—in those days, the only road out of the village, winding around the foot of the mountain through Lower and Inner Togawa.

"If that kid were in school today," Grandma Kiyoko said, "He'd ride the short bus."

A month after his release from hospital, Uncle Shigenori appeared in our garden resembling an overgrown embryo: hands on his hips, puckered smile in head like a shrivelled peach, belly pinched to nothing by the purlicue of his spine. Over his shoulder I saw Grandma Kimie tottering up the path from the car park. I noticed the diesel-powered tiller in the bed of the kei-truck, but didn't immediately register the implication.

"Our tomatoes are pathetic so far," I said by way of greeting. I blamed a series of heavy showers that had come a month before the rainy season, pointed to the newest fruits already rotting before they were ripe.

From what I could gather, Uncle Shigenori was saying I'd planted the seedlings too shallow—that all the hairs on the stalk would've grown to roots if I'd buried them—and that I had to pinch off the suckers between the branches.

Grandma Kimie plucked a thoroughly rotten cherry tomato from the vine and popped it in her mouth.

"Isn't it sour?" I asked.

"Hennh?"

At that point Anna took over the conversation in dialect—and continued speaking that way after Togawa had wandered back to the *kei*-truck.

"Do you have to speak that way?" I asked.

"If you don't speak the dialect, they won't understand you."

"If you don't speak standard Japanese, I won't understand you."

She laughed and bent down with her trowel to dig between the previous year's spring onions. On the other side of the garden, Uncle Shigenori was revving his motor.

My heart sank. "He's not going to plough now, is he?"

"Just let him do it," she sighed. "I told him to avoid the perennials."

When I turned around, he was driving straight through the kale patch, macerating the seedlings. I rushed into the patch screaming.

Uncle Shigenori glanced up at me with a look of vague uncertainty, but kept on ploughing. I looked to my wife in desperation.

"There's nothing to be done about it," she said.

Grandma Kimie marched toward us with a frown, commanding Anna to pull apart any spring onions that could be separated and plant each of the smaller shoots in its own space. One by one she tossed the larger stalks onto the path.

"Let me clean those," Anna said. "I'm going to bring them to the kitchen."

Grandma Kimie declared in a tone that admitted no argument, "You can't eat those."

"We always eat those," my wife said lightly.

"Hennh?"

As far as I could tell, Togawa never ate vegetables unless they were soaked in sugar and vinegar. We visited their house once, after Hirō-san's ten-year memorial service. From an entryway cluttered with rubbish bins, kerosene tanks, rusted spray cans and decaying shoes, we were led through a sitting room where every chair and sofa was piled with months of unwashed, fly-ridden laundry. We sat on the floor before a low table, a priest read a sutra from an accordion book older than our house, and for lunch they served a platter of soggy tempura and inari-zushi from a discount supermarket.

I carried the smallest of the spring onions to the kabocha patch. In a strip along the edge of the path I sculpted a mound from the soil Uncle Shigenori had churned up. At my shoulder, Grandma Kimie was insisting (as far as I could gather) that green onions are planted by making two mounds, laying the stalks roots-down between them, and pushing the mounds together.

"We don't have that much space," I objected.

"Hennh?"

"We need to make just one mound. To leave enough room for the kabocha."

"*Hennh?*"

"Let her do it the way she wants," my wife said. "We can fix it later."

I clenched my teeth and watched Grandma Kimie build two overly wide mounds. When their length was four times what I'd planned, I could hold back no longer and begged my wife to distract her. Once her back was turned I set to sculpting a single row. She was back at my side in an instant.

"No, no, no, not like that!" One after another, she yanked out every shoot I'd planted.

"Please!" I cried. "Please, just stop!"

Grandma Kimie looked at me aghast, then stormed off to the *kei*-truck.

Uncle Shigenori dipped his head with a trembling smile. "Sorry about that."

In the daylight that remained after Togawa's departure, we raked and levelled the garden beds, chopping unearthed chunks of clay and rebuilding each of the mounds. By the time all was ready to be re-planted, my nerves had calmed enough to wonder if Grandma Kimie would forgive my outburst.

"She'll be fine," my wife said. She'll probably make a joke out of it: 'Hey, how are those spring onions doing?'"

The sky had turned shades of pink and lavender streaked with feathery auriferous clouds. I was thinking of how far we'd come, how much we'd improved the building and its grounds, of the soil caked on my knees and my T-shirt soaked with sweat and stinking of ammonia, and how good a hot shower was going to feel.

Even Anna forgot that we should've been inside. Looking past me toward the figures on the road, the serenity in her face turned to fear.

Anna calls them *ano hito-tachi*—"those people"—although in the twilight they don't always look like people. It was a morbid curiosity that made my eyes linger the first time I saw them. I could make out only the shapes of their preternaturally thin bodies, black but for each pair of greyish legs, lacking any visible flesh or discernible heads, and all plodding forward with the same terrible slowness.

I hurried after my wife into the house. She bolted the door and stood motionless in the entryway, as though counting the seconds and minutes for "those people" to pass. Many times I'd wondered what might happen if one of them were to veer from the march, to come up our path and ring our doorbell. What if, I wondered, I set aside my fear and dared to wave at them?

My wife's father was born missing an entire hemisphere of his brain. In his early childhood the gap filled with fluid and the remaining hemisphere took over all functions of the whole. He graduated from the faculty of Electronics and Information Technology at Tokyo Polytechnic, married young, and went to work as an engineer at Panasonic. Before I met him a decade ago I heard he'd inexplicably quit his job at the height of his career to work as a delivery driver, had enrolled the family in a new religion called Law of the Soul, and frequently fell off his bicycle, but to all other appearances he was normal.

He invited me out for okonomiyaki. I expected his first question to be, "What makes you think you're good enough for my daughter?" Instead, he told me how much he loved "vegetable" (by which, I later learned, he meant cabbage) and asked me point blank if we were going to get married.

"Erm—well—we haven't really discussed it ..."

He slicked into the okonomiyaki, shrugged and smiled. "Up to you," he said. (The actual expression he used was *futari no mondai*, which I thought meant something more like "your problem," until my wife laughingly corrected me.)

Walking back to the house, he moved so slowly he was almost graceful, a wiry little man with tiny black eyes, scant grey hair and tiny, widely-spaced teeth that protruded when he laughed.

"Your father is cute," I said.

"Everyone thinks so," Anna said, "Until they get to know him."

The next time he fell off his bicycle he landed on his head. Predicting an aneurysm sooner rather than later, the doctors forbade him to ride. I chanced into him downtown on a blustery autumn afternoon and asked if he was all right. Laughing his gently wheezing laugh, he chalked it all up to age. Not long thereafter, even his walking speed slowed to where ambling to town was no longer practical. He lingered between his bedroom and the downstairs sofa, and reverted to his old habit of chopping cabbage at the kitchen counter after the dinner dishes had been cleared, exasperating Emi the way it had exasperated Setsuko—"There wasn't enough vegetable," he'd shrug. He began to forget he was retired. He'd get up suddenly and announce he had to go to work. He had seizures and forgot his own name. He defecated in his clothing. Once, when Emi wasn't there to watch him, he wandered out into the street pushing the wheeled pole slung with his catheter bag. He'd reached the shopping district before a stranger picked him up and drove him back to the address printed on his health insurance card.

The care home is just off the main highway, accessible via a tunnelled underpass to a carpark more crabgrass than asphalt. To reach the grounds, you cross a plank over a ditch to the cement stairs and head past the long tinted veranda windows of the wing where Grandma Kiyoko lives. You push through the front door, and it locks behind you—to exit, you have to type in the code on the placard taped above the punch pad.

My wife went with Emi in June to move her father into the home, and visited him there days later. At the end of several confusing lengths of corridor, surrounded by half a dozen aides in masks and scrubs, he sat bobbing his head among the motionless staring aged.

"Father," Anna called.

Still bobbing his head, he intoned a string of generic pleasantries, not a spark of recognition in his tiny eyes.

"Father," she said. "It's me."

"Setsuko? Is that you?"

"It's Anna, Father."

"Impossible," he said. "Anna doesn't have all those wrinkles."

"It's amazing Buyo turned out so normal," my wife said after that visit. Buyo is her nickname for her sister, an onomatopoeia for the jiggling collops of flesh she's gained by living alone. By "normal," she meant average for a Japanese woman of the age cohort: Emi wears a uniform to work, is crazy about Arashi, finds foreign confections utterly unpalatable, and has no political opinions whatsoever.

"She hardly grinds her teeth anymore," Anna said, "Thanks to the medication."

When the sisters and their father still lived together, Anna was kept awake at night by the incessant scraping, rasping racket from Emi's room. Emi slept with a plastic guard in her mouth, but when it didn't fall out she chewed through it. Anna sat up till dawn thinking of colonies of rats gnawing through the walls, burgeoning, multiplying till they filled every crevice, finding no object hard enough to satisfy those thousands of sets of teeth. Anna pushed aside her bed and dresser and vanity to dab shades of green acrylic into the fibres of tiny leaves, one by one, till her four walls were a deciduous forest. Buzzing till daylight with cigarettes and espresso, she slept into the afternoon, rising once for a single serving of white rice sprinkled with *furikake*. By the time we met she weighed barely six stone.

She told me all about her family on her first date, by way of making clear how, back then, she was still set against any ideas of marriage or children. She'd be a terrible wife and mother, she said, and there could be no question of breastfeeding with the amount of antipsychotics in her bloodstream.

"I'm crazy," she said.

Her father's family were the oldest Shinto clergy in the region, sent from Nara by the shogun to establish the shrines. The youngest of eight sons, Anna's father gambled away his inheritance at pachinko and mahjongg, and spent the remainder to furnish the largest room in their new house with the tiered tables, iron bodhisattva statues, white faience orchid vases and platters to pile with the evergreen branches required for the ceremonies of Law of the Soul. From the time they were in kindergarten, Anna and Emi were taught to kneel and pray at the altar without the faintest idea what it was to which they were praying or why.

Sometime in primary school, Anna asked her mother why she'd decided to have children. "To have someone to take care of me in my old age," was the answer.

In Anna's third year of high school, she came home to find her mother's corpse dangling in a noose from the rafters.

"She was crazy, too," Anna said.

After the funeral, her father travelled to Law of the Soul headquarters in Kobe for a special consultation with one of the highest-ranking shamans. He returned with the declaration that the house was cursed.

"We're moving," he said.

I asked my wife if she ever resented being forced to abandon the house she'd grown up in.

"You want to live in a *kominka* where the roof leaks and centipedes and spiders drop onto your head while you're sleeping?" she laughed. "You can have it."

Naturally, Grandma Kiyoko paid for the second house.

Emi had been having the time of her life at university, cross-breeding cacti in the laboratory and having onigiri-eating contests with her dorm mates. She even had a boyfriend—apparently, the only one she ever had. After she heard the news, she struggled through her senior year and returned to live in what had been the new house, where she remains.

"Don't you ever feel lonely?" I once asked her.

Emi's eyes and mouth became perfect circles as she whipped her face side to side. "No! Never!"

I watched those figures, *ano hito-tachi*, pass in the road for the last time this summer. I counted them as they passed, until I lost count, and wondered if it were for any reason other than my wife's better instincts that their appearance filled me with foreboding. I wondered what could be the worst that might happen if one did come up our path to visit us.

The following day, Uncle Shigenori lost his vision on the prefectural highway. The way he described it to Anna, everything suddenly clouded over, leaving a huge lacuna of obscurity in the centre of his field of vision even when the rest of the image returned. He pulled onto the shoulder and waited, the obscurity descending and lifting in waves. After what Anna guesses was probably an hour or more, he called his nieces. Emi drove to our house to collect Anna. With the help of GPS they located the *kei*-truck, took Uncle Shigenori to the hospital, then drove him home.

"Uncle Shigenori's IQ is lower than we thought," Anna said when she came home.

"What, did they test that at the hospital?" I asked.

"No, but his truck is full of coins. The glove box and ash tray are stuffed with them. They're all over the dashboard. I don't think he uses coins at all. I don't think he can count them. He probably pays for everything with bills and tosses the change any old place."

She also said she had a moment with him in the garden while Emi was inside with Grandma Kimie, and that he was waxing generous about a piece of unused land that remained in the family, a tract of wild brush on a mountain road built onto the only ledge between the weald and the ravine. Anna had mentioned before that we might like to grow nut trees. Uncle Shigenori promised to drive us out to survey the land when his vision returned and, come November, to dig his brush clearing machine from storage and help us with the planting.

Inside, Grandma Kimie was telling Emi something had to be done about Uncle Shigenori's drinking and his outbursts of violence.

"You don't mean he's hitting her?"

"I mean he's hitting her." Anna said it like she was already resigned to the situation, but she said she'd talk to Grandma Kiyoko about it.

Grandma Kiyoko lost the use of her legs last year. If patterns hold, her mind isn't far behind. She was walking when I first met her—she came to visit us at the flat we were renting while we searched for a house— and promised that no matter how far her body decayed, she'd never go senile. When her energy was high she rambled incessantly without ever coming to the purpose. It took her years to remember my name. I was always *kono kare*—"this guy." She surprised my wife by calling me by name when we went to pack her unworn clothes and other scant belongings to transport from one wing of the care home to another where she'd have more supervision. In the midst of the pandemic, the home was closed to visitors, leaving her with little stimulation besides the television. When they finally let us see her again, she could no longer roll herself over.

Anna had bought her a mobile telephone—the old-fashioned kind, on the assumption that it would be easier to comprehend than a smartphone.

Anna and Emi received pocket calls and empty text messages. When they texted Grandma Kiyoko, she couldn't see the screen; when they called she couldn't figure out how to answer.

She flipped her chin toward where the phone lay on her bedside table. "Take it away."

Anna moved the phone further back, optimistically leaving it within Grandma Kiyoko's line of vision.

Grandma flipped her chin at the unread novel and address book now before her eyes. "Take those away too."

When Anna moved those, the only thing remaining was the little electric clock.

"Take that away too."

"There will be nothing on the table."

"Take it away."

One of the smocked attendants lurked in the doorway. Anna had more than once, when coming to visit, caught the staff milling idly about while Grandma Kiyoko called feebly out to them.

"Uncle Shigenori's been hitting Grandma Kimie," Anna said at length.

"Figures," Grandma Kiyoko said. "Hirō-san used to beat the hell out of her too."

I gazed out the window at a tiny neglected quadrangle between the fence and the wings of the building. I thought of all the residents, Anna's father included, with no view of the outside world but overgrown weeds, listening daily to the violent coughs of the dying, inhaling the odours of their own putrefying flesh and excrement.

"Can't anyone come to pull up the weeds?" I asked.

A flock of sparrows descended on the ragged patch. In an instant they picked the foxtails clean of seeds, then disappeared into the sky.

The cypress forest opened on the last stretch before Togawa. Shreds of gossamer fog drifted over fir trees bent like a throng of nameless beasts with the weight of rain. The wide creek ran in patches of froth, tugging its mugwort bushes toward the inclines. I thought of our village built around the rice paddies and the space for its shrine cut squarely into the middle, obscured from the road by a grove of maples centuries old. I recounted the seven years we've lived in our village, and reflected that it was only by the grace of time that I felt at home. I thought of the beauty in the decay of the Togawa house, in the broken concrete path to the house and the patina of wet moss on the foundation, in the scores of broken and weed-filled flower pots that littered the trampled courtyard, itself steadily reclaimed by thickets of mugwort and chameleon plant.

Uncle Shigenori bobbed his head and said Grandma Kimie was sleeping. He called to her up the stairwell: "Oi! Oi!"

I expected Grandma Kimie to hobble down the stairs with one side of her head mashed by the pillow, a lopsided smile on her crinkled face.

"Oi! Oi!"

I tried to recall the names of the random flowers wilting in their pots among the stronger tufts of weeds that geysered through the rifts in the foundation.

Uncle Shigenori staggered up the stairs, still calling for Grandma Kimie.

My wife had been upstairs just once. The rooms and corridors, she said, were crammed with unsorted trash. She'd hauled out carloads of clothes more mould than fabric, and boxes upon boxes of objects obscured by decades of grime. I thought of the empty and decaying houses in our neighbourhood, of entire decaying districts along the rivers, and of the thousands, the tens of thousands, of others across Japan.

I turned to Anna. Her eyes fixed on the doorway. An ethereal creaking rose from the second storey. Anna dashed inside. As her footsteps beat the stairs the wailing reached its crescendo. Only then did I recognize it as a human voice.

The trees around me teemed with the tiny chirps of birds, and with the first hint of the cicadas' whirring hum, a sound that would, before long, overpower all others.

Shakeema Edwards

New Mexico Whiptail Lizards

are parthenogenic. In grassland-bordered desert,
the heat of sand against her slender body,
a female replicates her chromosomes alone,
orchestrating whole genomes. Through virgin birth,
she bears daughters identical to herself—
clones unconcerned with inheriting her pale-blue tinge,
her brown and yellow stripes, her spottiness,
knowing in their nascence they are their mother.

Shakeema Edwards

The Mating Behavior of Burying Beetles

He meets her near a hedge of hydrangeas,
where a blackbird has landed after falling
from a telephone pole. Its body cools as it waits
for them to make a place for it below loosened soil.
Together, they preen it, feather by feather—as its mother had
when it was still in nest—and embalm it with honey-
colored spit. They mate and make its corpse a sacrament
for their nursery. So when their tenerals emerge in June,
it feels the air under their hindwings.

Aoife Riach

New Year's Resolutions

My borders are bleeding again,
staining things that should be separate.
World War Three chat in the canteen and probably
could feel something but just want to watch
this man eat cake, calibrate his eye colour
in January noonlight. Cathedral's dressed in
scaffolding, rather be whipped around
in the weather warning or dismantled word
by word than unslot Jengas and stack slats
into clear and incontestable reflections.

If poems are prayers, what do I worship?
Asked for tomatoes in this sandwich
only to pick each pink sponge out.

Emilia Ong

Careful

This may never have occurred to you, either in life or in mind, but let me tell you, it is a very odd experience to be sitting on a bench surrounded by men eating an apple. The men weren't eating the apple, I was. I was listening to the lap of the ocean you see, and I wouldn't have bought the apple because so often here they are crumpled like used brown paper bags, fitfully lined and quiltedly squishy, but I just thought I'd check in Big Mart, and what do you know, on the one day I wasn't desperate for an apple, there were two sitting there on top of the mound – rather a shambolic hillock, I must say, and one whose stack had been built up inside a dangerously tilted crate (tilted, I suppose, for ease of access, though neither the tilting nor the stacking has ever struck me as a particularly conducive way to store apples, given that these choice items of Nature's bounty are so feebly susceptible to harbouring the tenacious signs of the knocks life has seen fit to serve them) – and they were, to boot, astonishingly unbruised and shining in that lustreless matte way which I prefer. They were the kind that are both green and red too, which I prefer. The ones that are only red – that deep shade, just like the blood which appears, I must confess, only every so often on my sanitary towels, and which consequently when dried I tend to hold up close to my face such that I might appreciate its glorious vegetal aroma before folding the towel in half and putting it in the bin, yes sticky side to sticky side and blood face out, and this even in a unisex cubicle because you see I no longer much care to protect the fearful sensibilities of men – have very tough skins, I find, and the all green ones in this alien country look almost yellow, like buttered potatoes, or like malformed lemons, or else like the lurid lime flavour icicle pops which have to be pushed up out of those clear plastic wrappers whose sides cut the sides of your mouth, for plastic is indeed basically a switchblade, so I find it difficult to get excited about those. Well, I dithered a little while, took in the prices of the other goods around the store – did I really want an apple, not to mention two; in fact, did I want anything at all? – but it was too good an opportunity to pass up. The two green-and-red apples cost around one hundred Lek, a much better price than at the flash grocers opposite the gas station, and it must have been my lucky day, because in front of me in the queue a dusky-haired white man was counting his money, and he had to remove two items from his basket which he could not afford. The cashier assisted him in suggesting that he take out a yoghurt and a tall baby-blue canister of deodorant, if I recall correctly, which he duly did without much complaint and without throwing any of the sort of lingering glances in the direction of the lost comestible that I would have done, had I found myself in his unfortunate position (I wouldn't have been bothered about the deodorant). He needed some left for tomorrow you see, that's what he said to the bulgy-eyed cashier, without a trace of embarrassment. Well this was a heartening exchange to behold, especially because the man was a tourist, and furthermore one wearing those special walking sandals with reinforced soles that look like they're sort of squelching out beneath the feet like irregular rice terraces, which meant that he was not really poor. I'm not the only one then, I thought: not the only one who counts when she doesn't need to. Who has to count, even though she doesn't need to. Who is (most of the time, except when I'm absolutely not) careful with their money and who is, because of this care, most of the time, humiliated.

As I say, the man however was not embarrassed, and so nor I think can we safely surmise was he humiliated. Humiliation, you see, only occurs when what has happened reaches into the pit of your soul and drags it out all naked and pimply with its hair uncombed and its stomach distended from its last mountainous meal for all to see. Humiliation only occurs when the beat by which your heart is kept marching leaps into your mouth and out onto the floor or onto the counter or into the lap of another and sits there throbbing away, disembodied and yet so very damningly bodily, while everyone looks on with horror and in disgust. This man wore the encounter lightly: he did not have the money to hand. Certainly he could have sourced more money for the next day, could have exchanged more Euros, could have done whatever it was he was in no mood to do. The situation was simple circumstance, happenstance; what have you. It was not the case that he could not put his own money into his hands. That is what I'm talking about: this was where we differed. Having but not having: a poverty of the soul: one with which I am afflicted and with which he, I believe, was not.

Being careful is humiliating because nobody likes a miser – either in money or in life. Often I am upset about money in this crazed country. You see, they round everything up in the most unmathematical of ways. For instance, if the price is 261 Lek, they will charge you 270 Lek. I am not able to ask whether this is normal practice because it is too degrading – too telling of my broken soul – for me to do so, so I still don't know if they do this because I am a foreigner who surely, they erroneously think, does not care for such pennies, or because that really is the nonsensical way of doing things here. To ask would in my case not be a question but an exposure, an exposure of the most repellent foibles of my psyche. So I pulp my query, compress my rage; by the time I get home, however, I often feel very sick indeed.

Worse is when they just don't give you your change. The other day the bill was 489 Lek. I gave the lady a 500, and she just smiled, and smiled, and waited for me to realise that I was supposed to walk away.

Still, it's better to be humiliated than broken. Or punished! I have had times of not being careful you see, times when I have permitted myself to spend with abandon, heedless of the figures which have totted ever so quickly up. I must tell you it is not a pleasant thing at all. When money comes out of me too effusively, so too does what it has purchased. Yes, everything leaks out in the end. I throw it away or dispose of it in some other wasteful manner. Which leads me to suppose that my money is not my money, and that what it buys me I do not subsequently own. Honestly this is rather a bind. I don't know how to get out of this fugitive existence. The point is that, bought or unbought, the world is never mine.

Then there's the way you have to gnaw at an especially big apple. Like an animal. Jaw open wide like a snap trap and then the unladylike clamping down. Have you seen the size of apples on the continent?

Quite incredible, let me tell you. These two were each larger than those pink grapefruits my father used to cut in half, one half for me, one half for him, and serve to us for breakfast on Saturdays. He liked them so I liked them too. He'd cut around the edges of the ruby flesh just where it collided with the chalky pith using a special knife which was curled at the end so that it got right in around the curvature of the fruit. The trick was to make sure the fleshy bit didn't detach completely but remained tethered by a thick cord lurking dutifully down in the murky apex of the grapefruit half's concavity. Because it was established, following my first failed attempt,that I was not good at preserving the affixed status of the grapefruit, I was never allowed to do the gentle knifing. I appreciated the rationale. I myself didn't enjoy trying to partake of my half of the grapefruit when every time I jabbed at it it spun coquettishly around like a freewheeling hussy.

Well I would never have imagined that I'd bring such a giant orb right up to my face and press it up against my tremulous lips, and certainly not in public, but there I was doing just that on the bench in full light of the fading day. As my teeth pierced the greenish-red apple skin juices spurted out in maybe three directions at once like leaping spiders, and aside from the sticky liquid which by way of said spurt came to anoint my cheeks and wrist and possibly forehead, the rest of the apple, being so large, was pressed up against my chin and nose. Well let me tell you I felt like one of those Siamese cats that my friend with three brothers owned for a certain interlude; she liked to remind me that it was a Very Expensive Cat, but it had such a flat face that whenever it ate its disgusting stinky food the brown mush would attach itself to its furred phizog, and when it lifted its head following degustation it was a pitiful sight to behold. Its fur in its untarnished state was already a muddy cream colour, like a mug of coffee prepared by someone who's been too stingy with the Nescafé, and this whole eating business of course just made it worse: to look at the rare feline after she had taken a moment to attend to her physical wellbeing was to be reminded of dishwater that's been sullied by a stack of unscraped Bolognese plates. After I took the first bite I glanced to the left and to the right and then towards the apple itself, yes I looked right at the bitten apple and at its grainy innards, which would have made me cross-eyed if it had been a normal-sized apple, but it didn't because this one was the size of Jupiter, and I discovered that I had left a sliver of skin dangling from the bottom arc of the jagged canyon whose circumference I had so boldly incised with my teeth. Honestly it had been quite a long time since I'd eaten an apple, because of the exacting requirements of my stomach I suppose, but as soon as I saw that nasty skin dangling all wet and browning rapidly along its underside I recalled all the apple-eating moments of my life and I shook my fists at yon there God and I cried out Why, why is it O God that I can never take a clean bite of my apple? What is so wrong with my teeth and why have you cursed me with such a faulty set of gnashers? Or is it my style of biting perhaps, in which case O God why is it that you have not taught me how to follow my sweet incursions through to tidy, irreproachable completion?

The dangling sliver repulsed me, but I could do little about it because of the men. I didn't want to pick it off and throw it into the sea and so draw attention to its existence. When I'd chosen the bench of course there'd been no one there. Before stopping at Big Mart I'd been up the hill again you see, up the hill which is near my house and beside my house, but not really near and not really beside, and it is not anyway my house. Well I'd just gone up again and come down again and it had been my third time up there, I had already firmly established it in my head you see that I liked the hill although of course I am rather wary of my likings and fondnesses at all moments because history has advised me to be so. My partialities are frequently not to be trusted you see, I'll tell you that at least. Well anyway, I liked the hill because as one walks up the road past the rogue coffee shops, each empty excepting a solitary patron drinking an espresso – usually an aged leather-faced man in jeans even in the most aspirationally-decorated establishments – and then past the dairy products factory, and then past the rival dairy products factory, and then over the forecourt of the car maintenance garage, which extends itself right across the pavement and whose virile youth stare unabashed at my person as I pass, hoses in their hands, and then alongside the arid display of the bathroom appliances showroom, one feels oneself to be leaving everything behind despite it all. Each step is a heave. The pedestrian footpath is broken in several places, not only by the garage, so I walk in the gutter for much of the way. Doing so is not a hassle, for walking in the gutter is anyway my tendency in cases unrelated to these and in cases undemanding of this strategy: it is one might say a morbid preference or a sick mirror of my quota of self-esteem. It's an absurd preference of course because at the same time I am the sort of person who likes things to be very clean, and so following every hill visit and the concomitant trawl through the dust-laden trench, through that pit for all the shit which is where I belong, through that ditch along the side of the road which is full of all the crap that the people zooming past in cars never have to bother with, I have to put my shoes in the washing machine. Because they are cheap shoes this is however playing a not disregardable degree of havoc with the sole and its glue, and therefore my hill-going habit and its outfall give me cause for concern during those quietest darkest moments of the still still night, when I do not wish to think of other, less tangible things. Well I heave myself up the hill bit by bit and with each step it feels like my being is being left just that little bit behind, like my being is a boulder in a sack in fact which I am electing not to take with me, no, not this time; this time I am leaving the boulder down there in the fracas where all the people are you see. And so, though I am undeniably still gripping at the sack as I heave-ho, what I am really doing is pulling at the matted fibres and stretching them out out out until eventually they'll break – of this I'm convinced. Yes, one day the sack will break in spite of its having proved to have been made of a very supple material thus far, and in spite of its having thus far been a sack which has never broken. For no, heavy as the boulder is and in spite of all my worldly meanderings and all of my other hill climbings – for yes there have been others – the sack has never broken.

 Eventually there's a turning because what I have not told you is that there is in fact a castle at the top of the hill. Manifestly that's where I'm going, and it's where the people all think I'm going, and thereby the sporadic stares (for yes there are always a few individuals lurking malevolently by the side of even the hill road) remain at a normal level and I don't receive any more China! greetings I think than I would down there in the town below. But you know what, in fact I'm not really interested in the castle at all. I couldn't give a flying fuck about the castle if you want to know, all I'm interested in is the actual slog up the hill. Or the mountain. Yes, I think it's a mountain really. And accordingly I'm not very interested when I get to the top either, and not even when I have completed the climb and am able to stand on the viewing platform with its broken binoculars and survey all the land like a king, which one would think would be an exhilarating experience but truly it is not, can I muster the remotest bit of interest. But even though I know this now, when I'm not at the top all I can think about is getting to the top, which shows you just how stupid I essentially really am. That said I do like the view of the other hill-mountains all crumpled around the back, they look like nothing so much as a sheet pushed down the mattress during sleep and this reminds me of so much you see, not least of my mother's bed, and the remembering makes me feel very good, very well indeed. It's a sort of connectedness.

And so of course I ate the foul sliver and all the slivers that followed, though I was mindful of the men and their possible probable gazes. I did not want to look disgusting you see, like I was slobbering all over my apple, though in fact it was hard for me to tell if I was or not because it was such a juicy apple. Juice or saliva was running all down my chin and the splatters had also attached themselves in dinky translucent hummocks to the rather large lenses of my plastic spectacles and because of this I had taken my spectacles off and lain them on my bag beside me on the bench. For some reason I was faintly afraid the wind would blow them away but I reasoned that though a tad strong perhaps, the wind was surely not cheeky enough to commit such a dastardly deed. So there I was, blind and eating an apple with three black figures – each wearing one of those awkward winter to spring coats whose scanty padding looks sparse and shoddily done, or maybe they were actually their winter coats, I don't know, this is a poor country, it's hard to tell what's deliberate - on two benches opposite me whose faces I couldn't make out. The sun was behind them because I had chosen the single bench facing the long afternoon rays, and this had been a triumph because on several preceding days I'd coveted this bench and found it perpetually taken but now I found that my securing of the favoured seat meant that I was spot-lit whereas they were in shadow and so I felt distinctly disadvantaged when it came to this unintended instance of finding myself thus garishly illuminated upon the social stage. I could hear the sea lapping gently around the stone platform to which all the benches were fastened. It was not a pier exactly but a kind of stub which departed only half-heartedly from the shore. Which wasn't a shore in the natural beachy sense that you may reasonably be imagining but a manmade esplanade with giant swirls and crude seashell designs embedded into the two-tone concrete. The concrete looked to me like someone'd been playing with the arrangement of their pate on a giant matzo cracker with no intention of eating it. People liked to walk up and down this matzo cracker at all times but especially between five and seven o'clock in the evening and just then it was oh around thirty-five minutes past six so it was rather busy. Then as now there would be families strolling companionably together and kids on bicycles and it was quite a lethal journey trying to get from A to B during these promenading hours. There were also lots of made up girls with tight black tops and rips in the knees of their jeans. And there were boys in figure-hugging tracksuits which, I thought, must be a new thing, and I felt glad of it because of course it is high time they got a taste of what it means to have to be body-conscious inside absurd clothes. I ate my apple as fast as I could. I wanted it to go away because of the possibility of the black figures' indiscernible stares. But then of course once I finished it I remembered that I had the second apple and that it was still snug in the plastic bag and reclining gently on the bench where I had placed it and once I'd remembered it I could not well forget about it. I didn't want to seem like a monster so I let some time pass. This was very difficult. I wanted to look at my phone because I thought this would look like a normal thing to do and perhaps I would not seem so darkly alone in this godforsaken wide world but my fingers were sticky and I didn't want to make myself and my belongings even more dirty just in order to look normal. That would be too high a price to pay, I concluded. And so I stared at the ground and at the discarded black and white shells of the sunflower seeds which had collected in the depressed grouting between the stones around my feet. The people here eat a lot of sunflower seeds in shells after taking them out of their shells and it is just like China in this way, which is funny because I feel this is perhaps a racist or simply closeted place and that they don't like Chinese people, a fact I can tell because of the stares and the greetings, and eating seeds strikes me as a very companionable and soothing way to pass the time but I myself don't do it because I have no one to break up a conversation with by way of the cracking and chewing of seeds and besides I have never quite got the knack of the cracking of the shell and extracting of the seed and therefore neither have I often managed to reach the ultimate goal of chewing because my mother never taught me, or because I am not really, properly Chinese.

And so I stared at the blueish sky to my left, though this of course meant looking in the polar opposite direction to the men and I didn't wish to appear hostile. Nor did I wish to appear friendly though so in the end there really was little place else for me to look but at the seedless husks on the ground.

Some time passed with difficulty. And then I thought fuck it and I took my second apple out of the plastic bag and I bit into it and what do you know the men stood up and went away. They must have been waiting for my bench I thought and now they could see that I was not going to be moving for a while what with this edible basketball in my hand still to be got through. I felt a ribbon of exhilaration then and then I felt mortifyingly exposed. Now I was all alone on the stubby outpost. Who does she think she is, I thought the people on the esplanade must be thinking, not giving up her seat. Taking up all that space as if she has a right to.

Susanna Lang

Crow and Anti-Crow

The crows started it.
One crow would make up
a brief poem, something like

>*No one*
>*owns*
>*the sky.*

The rule was
the next crow
had to contradict the first:

>*Crows*
>*own*
>*the air*
>*they speak into.*

A person who wasn't
a crow
but knew the language, added

>*The axe*
>*owns*
>*the branch*
>*where the crow sits.*

Then translated the poem
into English
and waited for an answer,
human or corvid,

while the crows
found another tree.

Hui Ran

seeing the flood for the first time

When I was in school
The vastness of things appeared
In books, on the page, on the square screen.
There were words for everything.
How corners fold into each other, how a feeling
Is a splinter in the rib.
I could line a face with my lessons.

Fast forward to the flood,
Only water, liquid and steady,
Sitting like a stubborn cat.
Do the lessons fold into paper boats,
Are they pliable for deft fingers,
Do they leap from print into a soaked plain
Thirsting like a sponge?

What is a fool's worthier errand? Is it the water
Or the napkin,
Or the soaking of the two, dissolution
Taking a leaf from physics,
Whether it is studied, or swam in, or swallowed,
Fissured or considered,
Whether sink, sip,
Whether a hole opens in the base of the cup,
Whether the fibres are worth drinking from.

Rose Malone

Tóraíocht: Scéal Ghráinne

ar nós Carol Ann Duffy

D'éirigh mé bréan den tóir: muidne ag rith
gach uile lá, agus deisceabail Fhionn go dlúth
ar ár sála; an bitseach Sceoling díogarnach
in ár ndiaidh, agus muid ag dreapadh thar
fallaí na tíre, is ag rith trí sraitheanna giolcaidh,
trí srutháin is claiseanna. Agus gach oíche!
Mura raibh Diarmuid athruithe in a ulcabhán,
bhí orainn luí le chéile i leaba clochach.
Bheadh duine dubh dóite de, fiú amháin
leis an leannán is fearr ar domhan.
Is féidir liomsa claochlú freisin:

D'iompaigh mé
I mo ghiorraí agus d'imigh liom ar mo chosa fada
gan smál ar bith a fhágaint ar an bhféar claonta.

Rose Malone

The Chase: Gráinne's Tale

after Carol Ann Duffy

I grew tired of the chase: always running
every single day, with Fionn's loyal followers
hot on our heels, that bitch Sceoling panting
at our backs and us climbing the walls and ditches of
the country, running through reed beds, through
streams and marshes. And every night!
If Diarmuid wasn't in the form of an owl,
we had to lie together on stony beds.
Anyone would tire of it, even
with the best lay in the land. I can change form too:

I took the body of the long-legged hare and away
with me. Not the slightest trace left behind
On the wind-bent grass.

Michael David Jewell

Camera Obscura

When I can't fall asleep
I stay up and watch late-night
reruns, invariably
conjuring your face
to the screen.

I try to find the right words, yet
they never come to mind.
I want you to sit here
beside me, although
you've gone into the next room,

saying that you need
to see clouds moving
across the sky,

rivers of melted snow rushing
down mountainsides
in spring, or an owl roosting
in a forked branch
while above it the moon
begins to rise.

These, however, remain elusive.
Perpetually receding,
they flicker fitfully

before going out, extinguished,
like phantoms trapped in a piece
of obsolete machinery,
and I am unable to tell
if I am inside

of a small round building
with an angled mirror at its apex,
or holding a darkened box
with a convex lens

for projecting an external image
into the world inside. I wonder if I am
the object or its outline,
and if there is even a difference
when I remember
the first time we met,

compared to how you look
when you walk out the door,
driving away in your car, its trunk
and back seat filled
with your suitcases
and the best half of our
book collection.

The trees on either side of the road
turn a deep shadowy green with
twilight, while a sharp-shinned
hawk circles overhead,
ignoring your departure.

MICHAEL DAVID JEWELL

Tina Pisco

Ring of Fire

The sky looks really hazy today. The fires are still far away but you can smell the smoke if you open a window. Not that I'm going to do that. It's over 120 degrees out there. The weather guy says that you could fry an egg on the sidewalk. I could go outside and give it a try. That could be my goal for the day – frying an egg on the sidewalk. Except that I'm taking the day off today. No goals. Just a day of lying on the sofa, triple screening and getting stoned.

The good thing about living with Eugene is that there is always some grass around. Eugene isn't really a dealer. He doesn't hang around in alleys, or at school gates or anything. He only sorts out his friends. Not that I'm with Eugene for the grass. I used to be crazy about him. We haven't actually had sex in months, but that's not the point.

The air quality has been terrible all month. They say that we should stay indoors. Wear a mask if we go outside. All my gigs have been cancelled. I don't mind. I don't like being in a room full of strangers anymore. Not since the bombing. I'll drive a half a mile out of my way to avoid passing the McDonald's where it happened.

We're not broke, but we're not rolling in it either. I'm still getting royalty checks on a song that got picked up by a coffee commercial last year. It's the one that I wrote about loving Eugene: *Until the End of Time*. We blew most of the licensing payment on a trip to Mexico, and a new car. The royalty checks pay the rent, but not much more. Eugene works part-time at the coffee shop. They've had to close the terrace because of the smoke, which has cut their capacity over a half, so he's probably going to lose his job. Things are going to get tight if the fires keep burning. Not exactly the best time to break up.

A Soul Hits playlist is streaming on the stereo, giving me a soft, homey feeling. The television is on mute, relaying the news in images and red tickertape running along the bottom; my computer is all set up to play some solitaire as I scroll through the feeds on my phone. If I'm in the zone, I can do all three at the same time. Four if you count the music. I can feel my brain split into tidy info packets streaming parallel feeds: Al Green singing, the clicking rhythm of the card game, the flow of memes and photographs as I scroll through my phone, quick eye flicks at the mute television: A road cordoned off by foreign looking police cars. A weather map with fires in bright red and orange. A close-up of a shoe floating down a flooded street. A screaming red BREAKING NEWS fills the TV screen. I turn up the volume.

"A man was swallowed by a large sinkhole as he waited for a bus," says the newscaster. I find this ridiculously funny. I laugh so hard that I start to cry. I can feel my face fighting to keep smiling. The corners of my mouth want to pull down, to open wide in a desperate howl. The sobs are lining up in my chest. Not now. Not now. I don't want to feel anything. Not now. I take the half smoked joint from the ashtray and spark up, filling my chest and smothering the sobs. The phone pings. A friend has sent me a clip of a black bear hanging out in an outdoor hot tub. He looks like a Hollywood mogul lounging in the water. I giggle, imagining that the bear has a gold medallion, a big cigar, and a cocktail with a little umbrella. Priceless. I hit Like, then change it to Love.

Eugene is gone for the day. He said where he was going, but I didn't bother to register. I miss him when he's gone, but I miss him most when he's around. Living with Eugene used to be wildly romantic. We were like two cartoon characters with red love hearts floating around us. We couldn't keep our hands off each other. "Get a room!", our friends would say, and we'd laugh. We could spend all night talking, limbs wrapped around each other, hands entwined. Now we talk about who forgot to buy lightbulbs, or whether to cook dinner or order in; our hands caressing our phones instead of each other. Ping! A picture of a cat in a tux. He looks dashing and seductive. I hesitate between Like and Laugh. I settle for the surprised emoji. Sometimes loving Eugene feels like waiting at a bus stop wondering if the last bus has gone.

The TV is flashing BREAKING NEWS again. Images of flames and blackened trees fill the screen. The reporter says that the fire is burning a football field-size of forest every minute in the Amazon. I'm not interested. I mute the TV and go back to my triple screens. We've got our own fires to worry about. Moving right along. Ready for some cuteness overload? #youbet #kittens

I hear his key in the door and I quickly put away the gear in the stash box. I don't know why. It's not like he would notice, or care if he did. The first thing he's going to do after putting the shopping away is to roll a joint. In fact, he'll probably plonk himself on the sofa and say: "I'll smoke one before I put the shopping away." Eugene is one of those people who narrates his every move. He's always telling you what he plans to do next. His declared plans require no verbal comment on my part. A nod, or a grunt will do. He's really only talking to himself.

Eugene drops the bag on the floor, plonks down on the sofa and starts to roll. "I'll have a joint and then I'll put the shopping away," he says. Before he sits down, he gives me a kiss on the top of my head. Like everything is great. Like we're still good. I look up, expecting more, but he's already busy lining up the gear in front of him. I go back to my phone.

"So, how's my girl?" he asks as he twists the grinder back and forth, getting the grass really fine. He always grinds for at least three whole minutes. It puts my teeth on edge.

"Am I still your girl?" I ask, still scrolling. "What does that even mean anymore?" I hate the way my voice sounds so whiny, so needy.

Eugene doesn't answer. Just keeps on grinding. He looks like he's thinking about my question. Like he's considering a really good answer, but he wants to compose it properly and get this rolling a joint out of the way before he speaks. My frustration is like a little ring of fire. I take slow shallow breaths so as not to fan the flames. All my built-up frustration could so easily ignite, burning what's left of us to a blackened crisp in an instant. I don't want to argue. Not today. I just want to love him like I used to.

Eugene sprinkles the grass into a long paper. He adds a bit of tobacco, licks the joint from top to bottom to seal it, lights it, and takes a long drag. Eugene closes his eyes as he holds the smoke in. He looks as if he is about to speak. When he does it turns into a cough, which makes him laugh, which makes him cough and punch his chest.

"That's some seriously good ganja," he says, blowing out puffs of smoke with every word. He takes two more long, slow tokes, and then passes me the joint. "I'm going to put away the shopping," he says as he gets up. "Then I'll have a shower. It's damn hot out there. Are you up for some classic Star Trek tonight?"

I pretend to be reading something and just nod. He pauses. I can feel him looking at me, willing me to speak. Then he turns into the kitchen without a word. Later, we sit side by side eating Chinese out of the box, heads bowed over our phones, as an old episode of Next Gen plays on the TV. Sometimes one of us reads something out loud. This is not a conversation. Just random bits of unrelated information. A list of headlines. We might as well be reading out the phone book.

I have the nightmare again. I am back in the toilet at McDonald's. My hand is poised to open the door. I can feel the fear as I reach for the doorknob, which is chrome and shiny. My hand is hovering over the doorknob. A dull thud resonates through my chest, deafens me from the inside out. The room starts to shake. The floor is trembling. I can't move. I hear screams and alarms. I need to open the door. I don't want to open the door.

I wake up in a cold sweat. I am alone. Eugene is in the living room watching porn or playing a game. Probably both. A siren wails in the distance making me cramp up all over. I can feel the panic rising. I think about my breathing, try to slow it down. Count to five. Look around. Find one thing you can see. One thing you can touch. One thing you can hear. One thing you can smell. Better. There's a short burst of tinny cheering from the living room. High Score! A car goes by, blaring disco. Happy music. Drag queen happy. I grab my phone and thumb it to life. I go straight to Netflix and log in. RuPaul's Drag Race has a new episode up. I click play.

I was in the toilet when that guy blew himself up. They don't really know why he did it. He wrote some crazy shit on a FB post that morning. Stuff about how MacDonald's was Satan's fast food. Stuff about feminists turning men gay so that they could take over, and how God was watching.

I'd left Eugene ordering at the counter. At first, I didn't know what happened. Just a really big noise with crashing and screaming. When I finally opened the door, the hallway was gone. The wall was gone. It was just smoke and dust. I could hear people crying out. A woman was shrieking. I had to find Eugene. Broken tables and chairs were piled up like barricades. People were buried under rubble. Some stood looking around like silent ghosts. There was carnage and chaos all around me and all I could think of was finding Eugene. I clambered over broken furniture. I pushed a woman away who grabbed at me as I walked by. I couldn't find him. I kept walking past people who were injured, looking for Eugene. Then I saw a little kid sitting on the floor covered in white dust. That stopped me. I picked up the kid and headed in a straight line, still searching for Eugene. I made it to the entrance. All the glass was shattered. The air cleared and I took deep breaths in. I kept walking until I was well away from the burning building. I could hear sirens in the distance coming closer. I stood in the parking lot, carrying the child, and waited for the ambulances to arrive. And as I stood there swaying, I thought I saw Eugene drive away in our shiny new car.

We go to dinner with our friends, Sally and Eliza, who live up in the hills. You can see the fire line from the house. Helicopters fly overhead.
    Sally and Eliza are vegans but they're good cooks, so I don't mind. Tonight, they've made a Lebanese inspired spread of hummus, flatbreads, crudités, and a big pot of spicy chickpea stew. I've brought two bottles of biodynamic wine and a bottle of organic Prosecco. Sally and Eliza always have loads of wine on hand, so it's going to be a boozy night. Eugene has brought a big bag of weed. Most of it is a delivery for Sally and Eliza, but there's a generous extra portion for the dinner party. We can crash in the spare room if we get too wasted to drive home.
    The Prosecco is to celebrate Sally and Eliza's engagement. They are getting married next year and are brimming with wedding plans. I have to dig deep to muster the celebratory enthusiasm required. Eugene laughs at something Eliza has said. It's his big hearty laugh. His I'm a little tipsy laugh. I used to love his laugh. I loved everything about him,

couldn't get enough of his smile, his smell, the feel of his skin. Can you still love someone when their laugh makes you cringe?

We talk about the fires. Sally and Eliza say they're not worried. They have a Go Bag packed and ready. Their campervan has a full gas tank and provisions for a month. They have been told to be ready to evacuate. If the wind turns the fire could be in their backyard in minutes. Eliza lectures us about the dangers of "normalcy bias." That's when things change so slowly that you accept the difference as normal, even if it's killing you. Or when they change so fast that you can't believe it's happening and all you can do is sit there repeating "I can't believe this!" In both cases you're fucked, because you're not seeing things the way they really are. You prefer to imagine that nothing has changed. That everything is A OK. You stay in your house as it burns down because you don't want to face the catastrophe of leaving.

"As soon as we get the word, we'll jump in the campervan and get the hell outta Dodge," says Sally. "This place is a rental. It can burn to the ground for all I care. We don't need much. As long as we have the dogs and each other …"

"And good Wi-Fi," Eliza cuts in, laughing. Sally cuffs her playfully and then kisses her as if Eliza's mouth was a delicious strawberry. Eliza kisses her back hard and then comes up for air, fanning herself like an antebellum Southern Belle. "My word! I think I need another drink to steady my nerves!" We all laugh. My laugh sounds hollow, but no one seems to notice, least of all Eugene. He is positively jovial.

"We always figured we'd go North, but they have fires up there as well this year. South is fucked and it's not looking great East. I guess we just have to head to anywhere that's not on fire," says Sally. For some reason this strikes us as hilariously funny.

"Where's that?" giggles Eliza, which sets us off guffawing even louder, "The ocean?" Eugene is slapping the table and hooting. Eliza and Sally are falling over each other. Our laughter comes in waves. It ebbs and then one of us repeats "The ocean?" and the laughter rolls back in, full force. I'm laughing too, though I don't think it's funny. It doesn't matter. It feels good to laugh.

Sally says she's going to hit the hay. Eugene has crashed in an armchair. Eliza and I sit on the sofa looking out the window at the orange glow that fills the night sky. She takes my hand and gives it a squeeze.

"How are you doing? How's your, you know? Your PTSD?" she asks, lowering her voice as if someone might overhear.

"I'm OK," I answer with a shrug. "I'll probably never go into a fast-food outlet again, but I can live with that."

Eliza chuckles and gives my hand another little squeeze. "I'm happy to see that things are good between you and Eugene again." I don't say anything. I want to tell her that things are not good with Eugene. That I'm pretty sure that they never will be.

"You went through a lot," she says, yawning. She closes her eyes, and in a few seconds, she's gently snoring. I roll a last joint before bed and sit watching Eugene as I smoke it, thinking about that day. The day he drove away and left me.

After I gave the kid to the paramedics, I tried to get back into the building to find Eugene. First responders had put up a cordon and wouldn't let me in. I knew that it couldn't have been him I saw driving away. Eugene would never leave me. I couldn't find the car. I was so confused. Nothing made sense except finding Eugene alive and well. I kept running up to people and telling them that my boyfriend was inside. That I had to find him. A cop finally took me aside and told me to go away and let them do their job. I called an Uber and went home. When I got there the door was open and the TV was blaring. Eugene was sitting on the floor smoking a joint. On the screen was an image of a woman holding a child in a parking lot in front of a burning, semi-collapsed building. I stood in the doorway looking at myself until my knees buckled and I started to shake.

"Why did you leave me?" The sound of my voice, so hurt, so shrill, crushed something solid, deep inside me. Like granite to gravel, in an instant.

"I don't know," said Eugene, his eyes starting to fill with tears. "I can't remember. I went to have a smoke in the car and then I was home. I don't remember what happened. I'm so sorry, Babe. I don't know what came over me. I guess I panicked."

"How could you run away and leave me?" My heart was beating so hard that my rib cage felt like it was going to explode.

Eugene pulled me up and tried to hug me. It felt as if I was being suffocated. It felt as if he wanted me to forgive him. I started shrieking "Don't touch me!" as I pushed him away. I beat my fists so hard on his chest that he fell back onto the floor. He didn't get up and try to comfort me. He didn't try to take care of me. He didn't even get me a glass of water. He just sat with his head in his hands, repeating "I'm sorry. I'm so sorry." He hasn't touched me since.

I've never told anybody that Eugene was at the McDonald's bombing. That he ran away and left me there. Only Eugene and I know, and we don't ever talk about it. I didn't even tell the trauma counselor I went to see. She kept talking about survivor guilt, but I know that has nothing to do with it. My problem isn't survivor guilt. My problem is that my heart is broken because the man I loved with every cell in my body is a coward who ran away when I needed him. That he has stayed away. I think about what Eliza said about the dangers of normalcy bias. This is my new normal, this parched pretense, and I can't fucking believe it. I leave Eugene asleep in the armchair and go sleep alone in the spare room.

The sky is red. Eugene is driving. The radio is playing *Until the End of Time*. I look over at Eugene to see if he's noticed. He keeps his eyes on the road.

"I can't stand that song anymore!" I snap. Eugene doesn't say anything. He is pretending he didn't hear me or the song. "I can't stand that song anymore," I say again, baiting a hook. I wiggle the worm, hoping he'll bite: "It brings back stuff I don't want to remember."

"No problem, Babe," he says with a smile. "Change the station if you want."

My pulse is pounding, racing up the steps of panic. My stomach cramps into a tight ball. I thought my heart was already broken beyond repair. Who knew that there were still bits left that could be cracked, splintered, ground to dust? I can feel my hands start to tremble and consider letting it all hang out. Having a full-blown, full-body-shaking, sobbing panic attack right there in the car. What if he pretends not to notice? What if he just keeps driving? I take slow deep breaths. Slow and loud, so that Eugene can hear. Look at the red sky. Feel the smooth dashboard. Smell the smoke creeping into the car despite the AC. I change the station, turn up the volume and listen to the news. Better. The winds have changed. The biggest fire is generating its own weather system. Hurricane strength. 95 mph gusts. 85% of the fires are uncontrolled. Funny how uncontrolled sounds so much better than out of control.

Eugene parks in front of our building. He keeps his hands on the steering wheel, his eyes straight ahead. "I love you," he says. "I know that things aren't great, but I still love you."

I can't bear to look at him. I fight the urge to start scrolling on my phone. Or hitting him. I stare out into the dark red light and say nothing.

"I miss you," he adds. He turns off the engine and gets out.

"I miss me, too," I say, watching him walk away.

The fires play *will they won't they* for three days. They've started cutting power for a few hours a day. The fires are fucking up the grid. That means no lights, no cooker, no AC. Our building has a generator, but they won't turn it on until we have a *real* emergency – whatever that means.

I bought a solar powered battery pack online to make sure that I can charge my phone. I didn't get one for Eugene even though he's always forgetting to charge his phone at night. There're so many things that I've stopped doing for him or making excuses for. The apartment is stifling. Eugene has left a note: *Going to do some deliveries. I'll pick up that shelf you wanted. Love you. Eugene.* What shelf? Did I say that I wanted a shelf? Maybe I did. I think I remember saying that a shelf in the bathroom would be handy. He's really scraping the bottom of the barrel to find ways to both please and avoid me. I guess he's coming back if he left a note. I'm never sure these days. Maybe Eugene is like one of those guys who goes out for a pack of cigarettes and disappears. I wonder how long it would take me to figure out that he was never coming home?

I strip down to a pair of shorts and a tank top. The TV is dead. I haven't turned on my computer for fear of draining the battery. The phone is fully charged, but I hesitate to use it in case the battery pack I bought won't charge again. I'm worried that it won't work if the smoke blots out the sun. I crack open a window to try and get a breeze, even if it smells of smoke, but after a few minutes I close it again. The smoke stings my eyes and tastes terrible. It can't be good to breathe.

I sit on the sofa and look at my phone lying blank on the table. Maybe I could read a book. Or play the guitar. I'd have a nap except I'm worried that the fires will come right up to the door while I sleep. Can you sleep through the Apocalypse? I roll a joint and smoke it, while I watch my silent phone and track the snail trail of sweat trickling between my breasts. Suddenly the phone comes to life, startling me. I pick it up and see that it's Sally.

"Hey girl. Did you see the news? It's evacuation time!" she says cheerfully. "We're heading to evacuation post number seven. It's on the beach. Meet us there."

"Eugene is out," I say. "He's got the car."

"OK. We'll swing by and pick you up," she says. "We got out of our place just in time. The roof is on fire. They're calling for an evacuation of the whole county. Grab your Go bag and meet us outside. Don't forget to take your mask and water bottles. We'll be there in ten."

I waste five minutes trying to decide what bag I should take. I waste another three deciding whether to call Eugene. When I do it goes straight to voicemail. In the end I just empty my gym bag, throw in a few clean clothes, my computer, and the six small water bottles in the refrigerator. I stand in the middle of the living room and look around at all our stuff. I can't decide what's worth saving apart from my notebook and my guitar. I leave everything else behind.

Outside it's scary hot and so hazy that I can barely see the road, which is lined bumper to bumper with traffic. My mask is uncomfortable and scratchy. My eyes are streaming. Little bits of black ash float in the air. The wind is picking up, shaking the shrubs and trees. I hear a horn beeping and see the campervan. Eliza waves as it pulls up to the curb. I slide back the door and am hit with a miraculous blast of cold air. Sally yells at me to get in. The two dogs are asleep on the sofa, so I sit on the floor, propped up against the kitchen unit. The cold AC is making me shiver as the sweat evaporates off my body.

Eliza keeps hitting the dash and murmuring "Come on. Come on!" to get the traffic to move faster. Sally is driving. She looks over her shoulder at me.

"Any news from Eugene?"

"His phone is off," I say, lying. I didn't leave a message. I didn't leave a note. It never crossed my mind.

"Don't worry about Eugene. He's a big boy. He can take care of himself."

The traffic is painfully slow. The sky has gone dark except for tiny lights flying around the windscreen like fireflies. I realise that they are embers. Sally curses loudly. Eliza suggests we cut across to the highway. Sally agrees. I rummage in my gym bag for a hoodie, but it looks like I didn't pack one. I sit shivering as we crawl through neighbourhoods where people are loading cars with children, suitcases, and boxes. One car has a mattress tied to the roof. A man struggles as he carries a large golden retriever down the street. I stand up to get a better view and see that the fires have gotten a lot closer. Giant flames are pluming above the trees in the near distance. A massive tower of smoke rises above them. We pass a hedge that is on fire. It reminds me of a picture in my Sunday school Bible of Moses and the burning bush.

Once we get on the highway, the traffic starts to flow, and the darkness lifts a bit. A pale strip of blue runs under the billow of black smoke in the sky. The trees on both sides of the road are sparking with tiny flames, while those further back are already blazing.

Up ahead is a tunnel. As we get closer, I can see smoke belching out of it. The traffic slows to a crawl and then stops as people figure out what to do. Two cars pull out, turn around and head back up the highway. The car at the top of the line revs its motor and then shoots into the gaping black hole. I feel the pull of inaction, so familiar to me now. I sit quietly marveling at the Eugene shaped hole in my life. I brace myself for the rising panic, but it doesn't come.

"I'm scared," whispers Eliza.

"We can't go back," Sally answers. She is biting her lip, hands clenched on the steering wheel, steeling herself. I kneel behind her. Put my hands on her shoulders and give her a little squeeze.

Sally plunges straight into the black mouth. The tunnel is dark and dense with smoke. I can't see more than a few feet of road. At the other end is a bright orange glow.

Joanne McCarthy

Garraíodóir

Shádh ár gcomharsan Catherine
a dá lámh in ithir ár gcúlghardín
's bheireadh sí ar mo bhosa beaga.

Tharraingíodh sí amach mé,
tráthnónta samhraidh na n-ochtóidí,
cailín nochta faoi sholas an lae.

Nithe gur thug sí dom: carbhat,
greannáin (Judy agus Mandy),
císte úll, sraith úrscéil eachtraíochta.

Dé Máirt, théimís chuig na gasóga,
mé seasta im' gheansaí glas
taobh le gasúir óga an pharóiste.

Ocht mbliana d'aois, ag campáil
ar an Oileán Mór, Corcaigh
pubail canbháis ina seasamh

aer úr na farraige á anáil agam
's léimeanna leathmheadar á ghlacadh,
thógas leí mo chéad chéimeanna.

Joanne McCarthy

Gardener

Our neighbour Catherine dug her hands
into the soil of our back garden
and grabbed onto my small palms.

She would pull me out,
summer afternoons in the eighties,
a girl exposed under the light of the day.

Things she gave me: a toggle and tie,
magazines (Judy and Mandy),
adventure books, apple pastries.

Tuesdays, we would head to Scouts
where I stood in green jumper,
side by side with the boys of the parish.

Eight years of age, on a camping trip
to Bere Island, County Cork,
the canvas tents pitched

and sea-air filling my lungs,
I made half-metre jumps about the place
and with her, took my first steps.

Lani O'Hanlon

A Café in Berlin

My flesh
is losing its grip
on my bones.

You have left
and I feel sure
you will not return.

On the walls, photographs
of leaves, lemon, gold, copper
with age spots – one–two–three.

A woman is chanting on the café Spotify
Srí bhagavati and I cannot escape
this moment.

Aum the women sing *Aum mm*
like the women
I danced with of every age.

When I was working in the hospital,
an artist weaved textiles
with the older patients.

I drank tea from a china cup,
an eighty year old man sang
I have often walked down this street before.

A woman losing her grip rocked
backwards and forwards "Oh my God"
she said over and over "Oh my God."

Lani O'Hanlon

Landscape of the Body

I haven't climbed through this tunnel of pink sienna
and moss green rocks to the secret beach in Ballymacart

for a long time now, to explore the cave where Susie danced
that day emerging from the darkness, drawing a chain

with her feet in the sand, a chord linking back to wombed cave.
So still she was in that moment.

Aisling on the cliff, a stream falling behind her, hennaed hair,
roots at the parting, lime striated through red pink stone.

Claire and Louise, balancing like herons in the sea.
I saw a bird in the rock, traced her wings. You can't fly

through stone I thought, but what did I know,
down on all fours digging in the sand.

You played the djembe and sang about a dragon,
Gwen lay back in the waves, her copper hair dark with sea.

Roman Vai

Conversation Starters for Therapy

Based on true outcomes of the 1989 Cleveland Balloon Launch

The rocks were more resilient than his corpse would be. How long would his shoe – the one he'd kicked off – remain among the ocean's debris? Would his body endure any longer, when it was tossed and scraped on the depths of the sea floor? After his eyes had rotted out? His mind would not step away from fear; fear for him held optimism and hope of prevention. His hope was of an immediate death. He wouldn't be granted one, he realized. The ocean had no sense of mercy. It had only the fantastic power to hasten his decomposition, to churn him out of the world with speed. But life would not slip out of him like a silk robe. He would strain and struggle only to fall among the sea's stones.

"Hold this here," said a voice coupled with a splash. Davis, treading beside him, sent a rush of water across Adam's cheeks. His hands were paddling forward, reaching toward something Adam couldn't see.

His view was of Davis working deftly at gathering some objects and discarding some others while paddling to stay afloat.

"Hold this one, I just have to find a few more without holes."

With strained effort, Davis handed over six objects that looked kelpy, like abused condoms. One of the slippery things unfurled in Adam's hand like a fortune-telling fish and became a small balloon.

Adam met Davis' eyes and saw a mixture of desperation and mania forming. He worried that the capsize might have caused them both concussions: why was the ocean's surface strewn with rubber balloons?

"Give me that one, it looks like it could still hold air," Davis said. He gave Adam a glance of conspiratorial encouragement, but he received a look he could not discern, something between ambition and delusion. Hiding in his glance was the improbable shared vision that they could both inflate these serendipitous balloons and tie them to their arms to rise from the water as their own saviors.

"It could be dangerous if you get tired," said Adam.

"I haven't smoked a cigarette in ten years, my spleen could hold against a tsunami. I can blow if you help me tie them. I can pinch and you hold. Don't pop them. Do you have sharp nails?"

"No, I bite them."

Adam considered how nice a cigarette would be. He briefly considered the beauty of choking on smoke rather than submitting to a wet death.

Davis, with a heroic effort, kicked to stay upright while he brought both his hands to his face. He gave deep exhales into a violet balloon and it swelled to retain his breath.

"Quickly, tie this one!"

He reached across the water to Adam, and didn't release his gaze until Adam contained the balloon in a knot. Relief washed over them both. Davis went back to skimming the water for more balloons with an athletic concentration.

Adam suggested they tie the first balloon to Davis, but Davis insisted that it would only impede his diving. Adam could use it, he said, to keep his arms floating and to prevent his hands from numbing.

The task engrossed Davis for several minutes. He was like a spear hunter searching through the water for a slow fish. Davis was so magnificent in the task that Adam forgot his own fear and a hysterical vigor took its place. How wonderful it was to remember how to fight for life!

He flung his head back and looked in disbelief as, one after another, limp, deflated balloons scattered among them from the sky. It was as if someone in a helicopter had come to distribute supplies, but arrived ill-equipped.

Adam could hear the high-pitched whine of a puncture. His optimism collapsed. The balloon couldn't hold weight anywhere near what was required to lift his limbs from the water. Davis dove further toward the rocky bottom, toward fate.

"What 'bout this one?" Adam said, pointing to an intact-looking balloon.

Davis sorted through the multi-colored debris, looking dissatisfied.

"Most of them have tears."

"We're bound to find one good one."

"If we had the tacklebox, maybe we could've repaired some ..." said Davis.

Adam stopped talking; his body was starting to feel heavy.

"It's important that we conserve our energy. It's probably better that we don't move much," Davis said.

Adam gave in slightly to the control of the water. His movements held an awareness of the weakening resistance of his muscles to the ocean; to its silent downward pull. He could feel the ocean swell and empty with him atop. Cradled above the tide, Adam felt as he imagined a fishing pole did: connected like an antenna to the life below. He could sense the carpets of moss, vortexes of sand, and the stony rock bottom.

Balloons dropped down, Davis looked up. None of them were useful. One stuck to Davis's cheek. He moved it with his tongue and bit at it.

"Maybe if I swallow it, it would inflate up inside of me," said Davis.

"That's one way of doing it."

"Have any better ideas?"

"I'd ask God that whatever miracle possessed him to fill the sky with balloons, that he could use that same power to bring us ashore," said Adam.

"I'd be miraculously disrespected if he didn't."

Adam kicked his legs up and tried to float on his back. Neither of them talked for a moment. To consider what would happen after the balloons finished dropping would have been a waste of breath anyway.

"You're going to tire yourself out. Try to float, stop diving."

"I'm fine," Davis said in a whispery voice.

Davis' breath was sounding more shallow, and his mouth was beginning to taste like blood. He could feel his muscles falling away. It was as if his torso detached and his limbs could separate and float off in chunks like a collision dummy.

"I'd say we have only time now," said Adam, floating supine.

"Sunset could bring a view of lighthouses."

"There's too many clouds."

"The clouds could pass."

"When the boat shows up, they'll know whose boat it is. They'll link it right to us."

"That boat is on the seafloor by now."

"It will wash up somewhere."

"Nobody is searching for us," Davis said with a tone that scared them both.

Adam let his legs sink down and started treading again. When he met Davis' eyes, he saw that the determination had left; within him was only dread.

"If we'd gone in on the varnish –"

"Or a radio."

"I've no care for a radio," Adam said. "I want a big plate of breaded chicken, pasta and tomato sauce topped with some parmesan."

Davis' inner fire had blown out. He stopped swimming.

"I'd take Casey for a walk. I'd tell him to go fetch some land."

"I bet he'd come back and lead us there without needing to rest," said Adam.

"You have to wait your whole life wondering how it'll end, and then the sky starts raining balloons like a circus, and you're using your skills from P.E. to stay afloat," said Adam.

Davis laughed and he coughed, and they both thanked god that the salty water obscured their faces so they couldn't see one another cry.

"You're good company Adam, you know? You're someone I'm proud to know."

"Don't swallow that balloon now."

Davis let his mouth fall slightly below the water's edge. Adam watched as Davis' lip touched the gray-green water; the hairs of his mustache spread on the surface and his smile refracted below. He bent himself down to let the water meet his ears.

"Don't be silly," Adam said.

His hand nudged Davis' chin back up.

"There are balloons falling from the sky. I never thought this, but maybe it's silly in the end. Maybe it was silly the whole time."

"I'm going to die silly."

He looked down at his hands and saw the refraction from the fleshy skin, alien, suspended in liquid from a laboratory. Had he used to identify this body, this thing, as himself? He viewed his kicking legs, the shoes he'd kicked off, the hairy arms speckled with sun spots: was this all he was?

"I don't want my heart to stop," said Davis, and Adam understood that time had closed in around them.

Davis paddled madly along the water, tossing balloons away from him at great speed.

"If my heart is straining, I know that I'm still alive. We can't rest. If we rest that's it."

"How about we take turns on our backs? We can each go so that one of us is resting and the other keeps watch?"

Davis looked to Adam and was met with a reciprocal gaze, one that held a united belief in their fantasy.

"I can tread first."

Tilting his body, Adam commanded himself to float. When his stomach breached the water, he felt the impressive weight of the ocean around him. It was like they were back to enacting the ritual of fishing: a search for life. He drew in breath to match the ocean's. He felt just as boundless, and as fluid, and as continuous.

"Do you want to switch?" he said, and waited for an answer.

"That's alright, I'll go in a minute."

The violet, half-inflated balloon swam up beside Adam, singing in a high-pitched whine from its knotted end.

"It has your voice," said Adam, laughing to himself. "Do you want to go now?" he said, and strained to hear the answer.

Darren Higgins

The Floating Bridge

In the lower field a blue heron stabs at a vole.

On the smooth round stones by the shore a painted turtle stretches its ancient thumbs toward the rain.

Gray zeros bloom on the water.

Imagine a light canoe made of bark and strung with animal gut, tight and light and strong,

its ribs holding us within it. This is how we'll cross.

Diarmuid Cawley

Antiquity on a fault line

Disasters are long
love like the weather

high pressure and low
you want me, you don't

I'm kind, I forget to be
mystery always works

amongst rude terms
language is clogged

only to be cleared
by the desert sunrise

to love or be loved
someone said once

love is an earthquake
making rubble of the heart

war eats heritage
monuments scarred

in the wind and sand
this isn't Ozymandias

no king of kings here, lone
sands find their own level.

Diarmuid Cawley

Ballyconnell, Sligo

Fishing cottages long tested
by blackest skies. Backs turned
against mobile homes fastened
with dripping rope gone green.
Undocumented flotsam caught
between howling lobster pots
where washed-out fields collide
with angular basalt—the skulls of sheep,
their rancid matted wool and skin
dragged on wire and wind.
Currents shifting, the abandoned island
divides the front, looking for answers
in the spray and boom; pollock at ease
in the stormed-out kelp.

John Kaufmann

Genesis 6–9

The rain falls in slants outside the window. It's been like that for days, and looks to continue for some time more. You have stopped looking at it, but you keep looking at it anyhow. There's a pile of dishes in the sink. Hardened gravy from last night, egg yolks from yesterday morning. You think you and the kids ate oatmeal this morning, but that might have been the morning before last. Shayala did not eat with you. You do not know what she ate for that breakfast, or the one before, or the one before that. The kids have taken the ticking out of the mattress on the top bunk and piled it in the closet in their room. On the tenth day, Shayala opened the door of the closet looking for a pair of rain boots and saw a solid mass of fiber, piled loosely from the ground to the ceiling filling the cavity of the closet. Breast-height, Tyler's hand emerged from the fiber mass and waved as Tyler and his brother, Kirby, cackled.

Tyler is eight. Kirby is six. Shayala is on the warpath.

You break the monotony of the waking part of the days with a piss and a hand-cleaning every forty-five minutes or so. On the way to the bathroom, you walk by the boys' room and look in. They have started in on Kirby's mattress now. Half a rectangle sits on the floor next to the bottom bunk bed. Joined to the half-rectangle an empty cloth envelope lies flaccid, like a spent balloon. You can't see what the boys have done with the ticking. You cross yourself and mutter a prayer, asking that Shayala not find out until the rain stops. But – from what you can see, it isn't going to stop.

On the third day of the rain, you called the gravel pit to tell Cump that you would not be coming in that day. Don't bother until this stops, he said. We have a swimming pool now, not a quarry. You said,

–If you get hungry in the woods, shoot an environmentalist.
–Heh.
–I need the hours.
–I need the business.

–This ain't rain. This is an act of *God*.

When the power, phone and Wi-Fi first went out, you found an old checkers board in the closet in the boys' room and taught them how to play. Shayala was still on the good meds then, so she sat with you and beat your *ass*, jumping three and four times and kinging four pieces. Dad, you *suck*, Tyler said. Kirby pointed at you and said, *Hah*-hah. Shayala smiled and lay back on the couch in her short-shorts and V-neck tee shirt. You were happy, because everyone was happy. Happy wife, you remembered, happy life. When it got dark, you told a story about the Rondaxe Man with a flashlight underneath your chin, shining up your nose. When you got to the point where the girl found out that the sound she had heard all night as she sat in her car waiting for her boyfriend to come back was his fingernails scratching against the roof because he had been cut to ribbons and hung up by his knees from a tree like a deer, you shouted *boo!* and the boys hid under the blanket on the couch.

You don't know if there are other board games stowed in the kids' closet. It's packed with mattress ticking now, so there is no sense looking for them.

It's not so bad, you tell yourself. It's not like we have to do anything. We just need to stay put. It's not as bad as when the power went off in the orphanage. When it got dark there, you would hear other kids jerking off at night. The priests would have you sit on their laps and pet you, or they would spank you if you didn't make your bed right. Even when Shayala gives you the silent treatment, even when the rain falls for three weeks and keeps going, this is better than that.

You didn't think you would ever find someone like Shayala. She has her moods, but so does everyone. Sometimes it's the woman thing, but you can't say that, unless you want to get your dick cut off. She worked the cash register at the Dollar General in Vernon when you first met. You liked the way her thumbs punched her phone and the way her neck tendons vibrated like an old-school piano when she laughed. You bought all kinds of shit just to talk to her. Beef jerky, chewing gum, underwear, mouse traps, caulk, tube socks, pliers, tape-measures. You put everything you bought in a box by your bed that you labeled "Chick at the Dollar

General." When you asked her if she wanted to listen to some music at the Robbers Roost, she smiled in a way that turned you to jelly and said, You didn't have to buy all that stuff to ask me out.

The first thing you noticed when you and Shayala set up house in the park was an old land-line phone standing next to the bank of mailboxes at the entrance. It stood attached to a post six feet from the power-line pole next to the mailboxes. It was sheltered by an egg-shaped, clear plastic shell large enough to cover one speaker, which was labeled "Telephone" in rainbow-colored letters. When Dee Dee, the park manager, showed you how to use the mailbox key, you asked, What is that phone? She said,

–It's been there forever.
–Who can use it?
–Anyone in the park.
–Where can it call?
–Anywhere.
–Is it free?
–If you pay your lot rent.

A week after you unpacked, you decided to give it a try. First, you called Shayala's sister, Jane, in Troy. Can you hear me, you asked. She said,
–Of course.
–This is free.
–What's up?
–I don't know.
–Well, call back when you have something to say.

Jane thought you were lazy and crazy. You never thought much of her, but you keep your mouth shut because you want to hold on to Shayala. Nothing's perfect, you think, but you remember being alone at the orphanage. I ain't doing that again, you think. No. Fucken. Way.

You used the phone to call the guy you called your cousin in Georgia and your half-sister in California. You used it to call Sammy Korda, the owner of the park. Everyone said Sammy was a prick because all he cared about was money. This is just money for him, Art, the cranky old bastard who lives near you, likes to say, but it is my fucken home. Korda lives down-state and visits once a month. You know he's in the park when you see his black Tesla with the sticker that reads There is No Planet B sitting next to Dee Dee's trailer. He doesn't really do anything when he visits except to knock on doors and ask people for lot rent. He never speaks with you except to dun you. I am late because my hours have been cut, you tell him, or because Kirby is sick, or because Shayala couldn't work because we couldn't get babysitting. I don't give a shit, he says when you say that. I don't give a shit about your stories. Dollar figure and date, he says. Dollar figure, date and nothing else. I am sure you are a decent guy, but that is neither here nor there. This is a business.

You used the land-line phone to call Korda because that way the call couldn't be traced. *Sammy*, you shouted the first time you called. *The potholes need to be filled.* Sammy said,

–Who is this?

–The roads are a mess and the septic is leaking. You can smell it from here.

–How'd you get this number?

–Are you going to fix it?

–Is that you, Junior?

When he said that, you clammed up, because your name really is Junior. Sammy continued,

–Could you put Shayala on, please? She is easy to talk to.

–It ain't legal, the way you let things slide.

–What do you want from me? Things fall apart.

–Fix them, then!

–I would wave a magic wand if I could, but I don't *have* a magic wand.

You also used the phone to call your father and the people who inhabited this land before white people like you came. Your father has been dead since you were two. He skipped out before you were born and you never knew him or anything about him. All you have from him is your name. When you speak with him, he says, Work hard. Take care of Shayala and take care of the kids, even if it is hard sometimes. Give them something you did not have. His voice is deep and soothing, like Darth Vader's. When you speak with the Indians, you don't hear anything. You look out toward the back of the park, away from the road. That is all wetlands, cattails, high grass and slack water, separated from the circle of homes that make up the park by a low berm. When you do that, you hear what you see through the receiver. You have never met an Indian in person. When you think of Indians, you always need to dream them up. Usually, you think of a man in his thirties, your age. Sometimes he looks like a Mexican in street clothes and sometimes he looks like Chief No Speakum Paleface Tongue, with a loin cloth, breeches and a headdress that sticks into the air and trails down his back. You think of his wife, parents, ancestors and kids too, but they are in the background. Mostly, you see him. The Indians used to live in the wetlands, but their absence lives there now. You do not have anything to say to them, but you call them anyhow. What comes out of your mouth when you hold the receiver to it doesn't sound like much – in fact, it doesn't sound like anything at all – but what you transmit is what you see when you look out past the circle of homes toward the wetland. Whether the Indians who are not there receive it is up to them.

Out the living room window, you see that water has breached the berm that separates the park from the wetlands and has formed a shallow swimming-pool, with an outlet at the entrance to the park from the main road. You ask Shayala, Can you call someone? She says,

–You're joking, right?

–Your med supply OK?

–I'm good. You good?

–I'm good.

When cell service first shut off, you walked over to the land-line phone and called 911. This was before the berms were breached. You didn't have to wade, but the mud sucked your feet in, ankle- and shin-deep. The dispatcher said, You mean the old trailer park near Verona? You said,

–Yes, Ma'am.

The sound of the rain on the awning was soothing even though it was, well, a flood. She said,

–We'll get to it when we can. Our own guys can't get in to work. Anything specific?

–Most people can't drive on the roads. If this keeps up, it will get into the well and the septic.

–We will get to it.

Yesterday, you waded out to the public phone again. You wanted to tell them that there was a foot or more of water on the park roads and that the water coming out of the tap now was the color of piss, but when you took the receiver off the hook, it was just dead air. *Severed*, you thought. You are on your own now. You need to proceed without guidance from your father or the Indians. When you returned to the home, water was lapping at the bottom step. Shayala had locked herself in the bedroom. Tyler and Kirby had found your toolbox and Tyler was showing Kirby how to disconnect the trap from underneath the kitchen sink.

You look outside, to check water levels. The lift station is submerged. Homes are arranged in a circle surrounding a ring road and, in the middle of the ring road, a green space the size of half a football field. The sewer mains run underneath the homes to a lift station at the part of the circle farthest from the road. From there, sludge is pumped into a large raised leach field fifteen feet high and flat on top, like a green mesa, that occupies most of the space inside the ring road. Shit flows downhill, Korda likes to say, but not in a manufactured housing community. Since the power went out, the lift station has not pumped. Sludge has accumulated there. For a day or so, you could see sludge seeping up from the ground above the tank. Now, the top of the tank is submerged and any sludge that may have been in it floats with everything else in the water that covers the roads and extends a foot up the side of the septic tumulus.

You look toward Eli Clarkson's home, at 15C. Water is halfway up the skirting. The soil that used to hold the elephant feet underneath the steps is gone and the porch sags, hanging off the home like a flap of flesh. *Eli!*, you shout.

Nothing.

Claude Easterdick lives in 11C. Claude has a buzz cut, a wandering left eye and a wife who speaks about how her brother-in-law has not been the same since he came back from Afghanistan. His home is slightly downhill from yours. Water occludes your view of the steps and porch. From what you can see, the water has reached the door-sill and is inside the home. *Claude!*, you shout. He sticks his head out, like a gopher. Hey! he says. You say,

–Hey.
–You good?
–I'm good.
–OK.
–Good, then.

Claude's shirt is sticking to his back but he looks the same as ever.

Art is paddling the streets in a camo-colored sit-on-top kayak. He looks pretty spry for seventy-five. He is wearing his porkpie hat, his button-down plaid shirt and the wraparound shades that make him look meaner than he is. His yard is now underwater and he has paddled up to the foot of your porch. He says,

–Kids good?
–They love this.
–I wish *I* could miss three weeks of school.
–Hah, hah.
–Hah, hah, hah.

You don't have a boat. You don't even have an inflatable pool float. Tyler has stripped the underside of the sink to the pipe stub sticking out of the wall and has disconnected the pieces of the trap pipe. Kirby is holding the curved trap itself and is pretending to smoke it, like the kind of pipe that holds smoke instead of water. You remember that you have an inflatable kiddie pool stored in the crawl-space behind the back steps. On hot summer days, you and Shayala would fill it from the hose bib. Ashley, from 31B, would come over with her daughter, Lulu, who was in Tyler's class at school. You would wet down a section of the lawn to make it into a Super Slide. After they ran and slid, they would jump into the pool. Lulu and Tyler would fill super-soakers, push up the window to Art's home and squirt them into his living room. You, Shayala, Ashley and the kids would hear a roar and then you would see Art burst out of his door carrying a baseball bat, screaming. More times than not, the three of you had smoked a blunt before the fun started, so you popped a blood vessel trying to keep from laughing. After Art went back inside, it sounded like a pressure cooker release, the three of you blowing snot through your noses and wheezing. Sometimes, after the kids were done playing, Ashley would say to the kids, Tyler! Kirby! Come to Aunt Ashley's trailer for lunch! And she would wink – you swear to God you saw a real wink – at you and Shayala. After that, you and Shayala would pile into the bedroom just the two of you and make that trailer *rock*. She was bigger than she had been before she had the kids and pale as a fish-belly all over, but she was big in the right places and everything felt right even if she looked like, well, a trailer park woman. You knew how to make noise, but what you liked the most was when you held both her hands above her head in both yours, looked her in the eye and rocked back and forth slowly inside of her. The time you spent doing that, you thought, did not count against your time on earth.

That's the kiddie pool.

The water is already thigh-deep when you climb down the back steps. It is maybe ten inches below the top rail that holds the skirting in place. It wouldn't be so bad, you think, if it were clear and not so damn cold, but it is the color of chocolate pudding and God-knows-what is floating in it, now that the lift station is dead. You pop up the top railing and slide three skirting panels out. You try to put them to the side, to keep for later, but when you look to the side and look back, you see that they have floated away.

Finding the pool is easy. You stick your head into the crawl-space as far as you can. Since the water is less than a foot from the diaper of the home, you can really only stick your nose. The pool is floating near where you had put it at the end of last summer. You stick your hand in, pull it out, half-swim to the base of the steps, open the door and walk inside. Shayala looks at you and says, What the hell are you going to do with that? You say,

–We might be able to store rainwater in it. We can't *drink* this shit.

–Where'd you find it?

–Where we put it.

Out the back door, you see a bunch of people have set up a camp on top of the septic mound. They have dug post-holes and sunk whatever lumber they can find – two-by-fours, four-by fours, you name it – and strung up tarps. Someone has broken the windows in the pole barn

where Korda keeps materials. Art paddles by so quietly you don't see him until he is right in front of you, resting his paddle on your porch. He says, Junior. Give us a hand. You stand up to go, look at Shayala and say,
 –If it gets over the top of the porch, take the kids to the mound.
 –Tyler! Kirby! Get over here!
 –I love you.
 –I love you, too.

Art's kayak is flat, open-topped and rotomolded. When you sit behind him, you think, Is it gay, sitting with a man's butt between my bent knees? But then, you think, The circumstances demand it. And who cares in a time like this, anyhow? We're all elbows and assholes now. You can't even see the top of the telephone when you paddle past it, toward the pole barn. Most of the landmarks are gone – the road is submerged, the mailboxes are underwater, the bulletin board supported by parallel four-by-fours that stood next to them is gone. The power pole that stood not far from the mailboxes is still there, and you can see the tops of the trees that used to guard the entrance. You stick your hand under the surface where you think the phone used to be, but feel nothing but water, some leaves, a little grit and a mass of something small and soft, floating. You think, My father and the Indians, and notice how, when you sweep your hand through the chocolate pudding, there is nothing to push off or bang against.

Korda keeps some spare materials on the rafters in the pole barn. The garage door is open. You paddle right through it, although you have to duck your heads to get in under the jamb. There are some pieces of R-board, quite a few skirting panels and a couple of OSB four-by-eights. The R-board is light but catches the wind. The skirting panels are awkward to carry on the boat. The OSB and a few waterlogged two-by-sixes are too heavy to move and probably won't float anyhow. You ask Art, Where's Korda? He says,
 –Counting his money.
 –I'll bet he's dry.
 –I'll bet he is.
 –Where's Ashley and Lulu?

–Gone, I heard. They left a week ago.

Art takes off his porkpie hat, wrings it out like a dishrag and puts it back on his head. You always forget how bald he is. He says,

–Dee Dee's gone, too.

–Where?

–I don't know. *Gone.*

By the time you get to the tumulus, water is less than a yard from the top. You and Art dump the material, make another run, and then another. Shayala, Kirby and Tyler help build a lean-to with a ridge-pole made of a two-by-four and a side made of skirting panels. A light wind blows the panels off. They collect the panels, replace them and tie them down. When you are on top of the tumulus unloading, you notice that the surface of the mound is squishy between your bare toes and smells like septic.

When you get to the pole barn on the third run, the water is above the garage door. Beside the gable-end of the pole barn, you tell Art to hold up a minute, you want to try something. You jump out of the kayak and dive through the now-submerged garage door. You can't open your eyes underwater. It wouldn't do any good if you did, anyhow, because the water is opaque, and you don't *want* to open your eyes or your mouth because God-knows-what is floating in it. You scrape the top of your head on the top of the jamb. Inside the pole barn, it is too dark to see much, but you can see that the water is already two inches above the rafters. You think, I can't punch a hole in this ceiling and I don't want to die here, so you duck back under, grab the side of Art's kayak, climb on and say, Fuck it.

By the time you get back to the mound for the last time, the water is a foot over the top. There are maybe twenty people there. Most you know only to wave to when you drive by their homes. You can't put any names to the faces. A few babies cry, but the older kids and the adults just stand, silent. Nobody bothers to speak. People have stopped building and do not bother to stand under existing tarps and lean-to roofs. When you climb off the kayak, Art collects his wife, Lynne, who has been standing next to Shayala. They paddle off, toward where you think Verona used to be.

Shayala has inflated the kiddie pool. It is too flimsy to hold an adult, but it is just buoyant enough to hold two small children, so long as they sit still and bail out the rain water. Tyler and Kirby sit in it. It bobs a bit, next to Shayala's knee, then her thigh, then her butt, then her waist, then her breasts. Tyler holds a toy plastic bucket and Kirby holds a plastic shovel. Keep dumping the water out as it comes in, Shayala tells Tyler. Do it like this. Be careful not to let the sharp part of the shovel bump into the side or the bottom. If you need to blow it up more, you do it using this – she points to the mouthpiece – but be very careful not to let any air out when you open it. Can you do that? Tyler nods and says,
 –Yes.
 –I love you, baby.
 –I love *you*, Mama.

She gives the pool a little shove and the two of you watch them as they drift away. They hover near you at first. Then, they float toward where the entrance used to be. Then, a soft wind takes them over the place where the berm used to separate the park from the wetlands. You lose sight of them somewhere over where the marshes used to be. The last you see of them, they are bobbing like a cork.

When the water rises above Shayala's breast-bone, you say, sit on my shoulders. You duck under the water, stick your head through and stand up. It is easier to hold her like this than it would be on dry land. You say, Can you see Verona from there? She says,
 –I can't see shit.
 –Do you see a bunch of dead Indians?
 –I feel like General Custer, if he were a girl on a rainy day.
 –Well, I feel like Sitting Bull.

You reach behind your head and encircle the small of her back with both your hands. She wraps her legs tighter around your neck as the water rises above your chin.

CHANNEL

Chinedu Gospel

If They Ask Me

after Camille T. Dungy

I'll tell them that the earth's DNA has
self-mutated again. & the oceans are still
suffering since the cyclone. Truth is, disaster
is also an invention & I've barred my poems
from clinging onto grief. At the atlantic shore,
a glacier melts into the blood of a sandpiper.
& two polar bears lose their polarity to spatial
distance. In another kingdom of living things,
various species are losing their specificity to fear.
If they ask me, I'll say day & night have
been harmful in particular ways. The latter
falls on me in the dark & the former breaks me
in the light. I'll tell them the difference between
brittle & broken is the weight of the breeze.
I'll tell them to touch the skin of a snail &
imagine mollusks without moisture. The earth
is denaturing itself. I'm digging into my
own thirst to touch a cold spring. If they ask me,
I'll tell them I have cried rhodopsin out of my eyes.
Beauty is just an imaginary line. Look, see? It's
morning, again. & the earth is already traveling
towards darkness. So what use is rhodopsin if we
only witness light to witness ruin? The earth
is ailed, & I read her a poem — O' stupid of me.
Honestly, I'd love to be more than just a sympathy.
We should be used to times like this, by now.
Bro, we should shoulder these burdens together
& pretend that the weight is bearable. The body
is unlearning too many things including itself. So,

at the dinner table, I gather the soft-bodied mollusks & annelids. & we dined deep into the dark making memories until the softest of us became the only memory. If they ask me, I'll tell them we all survived, yes, we fucking did.

Morgan Leathem Ventura

Aquatic Dirge

Above the massive ruin, an abode of spirits,
a relinquished reliquary.
The archaeologist jabs a finger at the ruin
and says in the past
there were "secondary" deities.
Imagine this, a stratigraphy of gods
      – god, we can be such assholes.
Given the chance, here I am
importuning what I imagine
to be tertiary gods,
lower underworld kind of gods,
or whatever may be dwelling
in the silt, the clay,
the soil beneath our feet.
We have no way of knowing anything,
all matters appear small
in the face of the monumental.
At night, a drunk man serenades me
and blesses the mound beneath my window
with his presence, his urine.
This does not defeat the chilled echo
ringing in my ears
every time my head hits the pillow.
A screeching cat at the end of a tin phone
reveals itself to be the pained, hollow voice
of a parched mountain yet to be named.
It calls out while the sky above swells,
and stray dogs stare at absent waterfalls,
pallid rain spirits, and sun-soaked architecture.
In our kitchen, the faucet fails to cooperate,

spitting brown, so we skip showers,
        so we skip flushing.
Back at the archaeological site,
eastern gale showers us with dust,
and the columns quiver and shake,
stone laughing while my mentor laments
the tourists and desiccated lizards littered
on the pyramidal steps.
Even the sparrows feel it, pulsing
in the thinnest of bones, the slightest of beaks.
A minerally sort of pining
        for water
past abundance,
future artifact.

John Tinneny

Corpán

Luigh síos ar an urlár.
Sínigh do chosa amach, agus ansin
do sciatháin.
Mothaigh an teach ag análú
i do thimpeall; an t-adhmad
á dhíosc, an téamh lárnach
ag crónán, mar an fhuil
i do chuislí.
Ionanálú. Easanálú. Machnamh
ar an lá a bhí.
Dean dearmad air.
Dún do shúile. Oscail do bhéal.
Ionanálú gach cáithnín aer
atá sa seomra ina bhfuil tú,
gach cáithnín deannaigh, gach leictreon,
gach baictéar fánach,
gach calóg chraicinn.
Ionanálú an tír. Cé a dúirt
nach mbeifeá ábalta brat a ithe?
Slog é, chomh maith leis na cnoic, na sléibhte,
an teorainn idir tusa agus an domhan.
Nuair a éiríonn tú, iarr do dhuine
amharc síos do scorn.
Feicfidh sé dorchadas,
Agus sa dorchadas,
Ollphléasc.

John Tinneny

Corpse

Lie down on the ground.
Stretch out your legs, and then
your arms.
Feel the house breathing
around you; the wood
creaking, the central heating
humming, like the blood
of your pulse.
Breathe in. Breathe out. Think
of the day that has been.
Forget about it.
Close your eyes, open your mouth.
Breathe in every particle of air
from the room that you are in,
every particle of dust, every electron,
every miniscule bacteria,
every flake of skin.
Breathe in the country. Who was it who said
that you can't eat a flag?
Swallow it, along with the hills, the mountains,
the border between you and the world.
When you rise, ask somebody to
look down your throat.
They will see darkness,
And within that darkness,
Creation.

Lucy Zhang

Reef Construction

Dad believes his manmade coral can replace the coral reefs that once grew by the island coastlines. He built a skeletal tree structure out of concrete and tied individual corals to its limbs. "Like ornaments," he says, although I think they look more like starfish hanging from a noose. The main structure doesn't feel very reef-like to me: an irregularly-shaped piece of concrete layered with veneers and coated with crushed calcium carbonate and cement. "Look at all these creases and ledges. Imagine how far the sunlight will reach and how much water will flow through interior spaces. Organisms will be colonizing these in no time," Dad tells me.

No one my age has seen natural-grown coral. The coral in the oceans turned white and soft, wilting and eventually dissolving. Dad says it was like watching a snowstorm thaw, leaving nothing but the empty, frozen floor behind. Today, coral only grows in fish tanks set at a constant temperature under the glow of blue spectrum light bulbs that substitute the sun. They feed on phytoplankton and krill and thawed frozen plankton.

Dad sets the structure on the car and we head to the coastline to deploy his contraption. He needs me to dive into the water and position it where there is the least amount of wildlife. We're supposed to be restoring areas, not intruding on others' homes. Dad insists it'll be obvious where to place the reef module even though the ocean floor is an empty wasteland without even rocks for landmarks.

"Why don't you head down? I'll steer the boat," I suggest.

"You know my legs stiffen up after a few minutes," Dad replies. I do know, but sometimes I think he'd rather be floundering underwater than seated on land with his eternal supply of cortisone injections and Norco pills. He's always talking about "heading down under," propelling through the water like you're flying.

"Pay attention to your fins," Dad warns. "You can snap the reef with a simple flap. Control your buoyancy. You might drown them if you kick up too much sand."

"Sure," I answer on autopilot. Dad thinks anything he builds lives and breathes and withers if you damage its self-esteem too much.

I jump into the ocean. Or more like, I push off from the boat and drop down like an anchor. Dad always says moving in the water is the most graceful sensation you can experience: water cushioning your squeaky limbs, slowing your gestures so you've got time to self-correct for clumsiness, blanketing your body without suffocating you. I don't know what he's talking about—inhale water and you'd drown and die.

I maneuver the fake coral reef tree to an empty spot on the ground, fiercely pushing and kicking to move the contraption, my hands grasping the structure's limbs so tightly I fear I might snap off some of the porous chunks of concrete. The boat casts a shadow on part of my body while the sun illuminates the rest of the way. I stabilize the reef's base, hoping it'll stay standing until the next time we visit. When I swim back to the surface, I propel myself as far as I can from the coral reef, taking a detour before reaching the air. The longer humans stick in one place, the more traumatized the place becomes.

"All set?" Dad asks as I climb back into the boat. I nod.

"I suspect we'll come back every month or so to check up on it," he continues. I think every month is too soon—the ocean is smarter than that, it won't guide anything to inhabit the reef module if it knows it's a human hotspot. But Dad goes on about our next trip, listing off the equipment he needs to measure this-and-that biomarker. *A wasteland is a wasteland*, I don't say.

*

At home, Dad returns to the garage, tinkering at his next coral reef monster. I retreat to my room where Dad thinks I'm studying for my qualifying exam for the Association of Environmental Engineers. Instead, I chat with Fasc1nate77 and Cyborg_Foo, two virtual friends I made while Dad used to spend several nights in a row at work, only dropping by to pick up packs of Instant Ramen and coffee pods. He's no longer capable of working so many hours without complaining about his back or hands seizing up, but when he isn't actively tinkering, he sits and stares with this unfazed gaze—I'm sure his brain is manifesting an invention of epic proportions.

Fasc1nate77 lives in the Forsaken City, one of the older cities that runs on gas and whose main sources of revenue are wheat, olives, and dates. Cyborg_Foo claims to live in the Metropolis, where you're either filthy rich with a house overlooking the coast or you live cramped in shared units built on top of metal trade-in stores. We think Cyborg_Foo is part of the rich even though he claims to be a Dirt Sweeper. He never complains about the water shortages or the regular power outages at nine p.m. or the rationed rice—one small bag a month, two if your household contains an expectant mother. Instead, Cyborg_Foo tells us about his encounters with street vendors—untangling puzzles made from metal chains, charming old ladies to give him a free bag of almond cookies, fooling snake charmers by distracting their snakes. "No one with that much free time and energy to bother others could be poor," Fascn1ate77 messaged me privately. I agreed, but replied, "You never know."

Dad and I live in a cottage far from stores and nuclear power plants, hidden by rows of trees on one side, barricaded by open water on the other. We moved here after he retired early, determined to get "closer to the crux of organisms." Once a month, I drive one and a half hours to the grocery store, which sells one type of apple—the red ones that've been genetically selected for their color instead of their taste—and a sparse selection of beans. Dad has lost most of his appetite except for a few random cravings for fried dough, and I've been subsisting on pots of mung bean and lily bulb and barley soup since before our move. Dad never had time to teach me to cook and I never bothered to invest more time in culinary self-improvement. The cottage sustains itself on solar power, and we pay a trivial tax because Dad claimed the place as a conservationist base rather than a personal home.

Cyborg_Foo thinks it's "so rad" we live in a cottage that looks like it's straight out of a "fairy woodland realm." Fasc1nate77 likes the pictures of all the vibrant greens and blues and red-browns of the landscape, but wonders "what's there to do?" "Not much," I confess. My home seems much less exciting than the cities, and I think they know it too, although they won't call my life outright boring.

"Help me with this," Dad shouts from below.

"What's wrong?" I call as I head downstairs.

"Concrete is too heavy. But I can't think of anything else as cheap and close to natural coral limestone," he contemplates.

"I could assemble smaller units underwater," I suggest. "It's just like piecing together a puzzle." I pick up several of the glass soju bottles scattered on the ground. "We could stick these in the main structure as coral securement points."

"Brilliant," Dad proclaims and stands. I rush over so he can lean on me, afraid he'll topple into the circular saw whose blade cover lies by the door. We walk up the stairs into the house, and then up another flight of stairs to his bedroom. He normally naps late afternoon before dinner. He claims there's too much life beating down at him in this cottage, but I think he's just compensating for all the sleepless nights he spent in the office.

After I help Dad change into his cotton t-shirt and draw the curtains, I return to the garage to chip away at the concrete. I hold a glass bottle on the base structure and mark its diameter. I rip a sheet of packing paper to sketch out new parts for a reef module that we'll be able to smoothly transport into the water and that I'll be able to reconstruct without needing to come up for an additional breath of air. It'll be so much lighter and more flexible than the previous concrete reef tree. Dad will feel like such a genius, a fellow to the fish, an ocean dweller unfettered by his pipe cleaner limbs.

Yoni Hammer-Kossoy & Abby Yucht

Deconstructing Babels
a lyric epistolary exploration

Dear A

Did you hear the jackals cry last night?
The air was looking glass still and I couldn't say

if they were down the street or kilometers away.
Piercing howls, cryptic. One moment you'd swear

they were mourning a lost mother and another
it's a party, like teens in a swing park
                      passing a bottle of arak.

The moon was a sliver past full so maybe those jackals
were surprised by the amber light when it slid

over a building. Maybe I dreamed it all.
Part of me is desperate to blur the lines between built

and wild, wants to stretch them like gum
and step through.
                    And then what?

Does it make any difference knowing nature goes on
despite all our efforts to break it? Sometimes I think

this city is what's left after an ocean
has drained away. That it's not jackals out there

but whale song set free from the bedrock,
that wind wishing through yellow brush is a tidal wave's ghost.

This stillness, this stifle, I know it's how seasons change
swinging from extremes until a new agreement settles in.

And I know change just is, as it always will be, but that doesn't soften
the unease it leaves behind in the night's fleeting shadows.

So tell me, please, how will we survive summer
                              after the jasmine vine withers?

Dear Y

I sometimes hear my neighbors cry, through the gap between buildings by the bathroom window. It gives me shivers, like a sudden change in nighttime air, this portal into distant lives, an excavation of drained oceans, imprints of mollusks on sandstone.

I live in satellite to many lives, here in Talpiot, but I cannot hear the jackals over trucks and speeding cars on Hebron Road. I anchor myself in the face in the looking glass, not to get swept away by speeding particles of humanity, this congestion, this pulsing ocean we tend to be.

Did you know? They want to take all these buildings and make them reach higher. In summertime, the top floor is already dense with rising heat.

In Talpiot, the jasmine intermingles with street garbage. The cats love it, but later the scent will ripen.

It is never entirely dark here, in the industrial zone. The clouds are tinged orange by streetlamps and window lights from tall buildings. When I glimpse the moon between buildings, it is a gift, and in a primordial shift, I wish I could howl.

Dear A

After the moon sets, there's a purple envelope of time
when birds come alive and bless the unfolding day.

Their songs invade my sleep until my sleep
becomes song and I can almost count them by name –

first a blackbird, then a mynah – but then I get lost
in sparrow chatter as if it's a passing rush hour crowd,

get lost in the crows trying to boss each other around.
I know they like tall lookouts, so maybe they paid

to push up the skyline? This pulsing ocean of humanity
always wants to go higher, so why not crows?

I say let's build more towers of babel if it'll save
some green space outside the city to play in.
                                              And then what?

Yes, back to that I'm afraid, it's a hazard of age, bright ideas
with no clear end. What's the point of saving something

just to ruin it later? This place breaks my heart one headline
by one, but I haven't figured out somewhere better to love.

In happier news, below the fold, tucked into a smudged corner,
I read that archeologists found a twelve-thousand-year-old whistle

made from bird bone, buried in the muck of a long gone
Hula valley settlement. Even so, they can't decide if it was used

for music, or hunting, or some other charm. They say
its sound matches cries of sparrowhawks and kestrels that even today

roam the sky searching for prey and I wonder what it must be like
to blow and feel the vibrations of their unanswered call.

Dear Y

Noises. So many damn noises, I feel like I'm drowning in them. It's the dryer that bangs on to the beat of a silent song, but the song could also be the voices that assault my ear, and the traffic and the water boiling and my car starting, and every moment of every day condensed into noise.

I'm glad you've been hearing birdsong, a shade of silence in a way. Do you mean there is peace that can be found here, in this city?

Imagine all the noise, of all the places and all the centuries, squeezed into a single space, the linchpin that is Jerusalem, the babel that is constructed and deconstructed at any given moment here. We come together and we collapse, like a burst eardrum.

Last Shabbat, I lay in the grass. And even there, I couldn't escape the rumble. Today, I considered going to the beach to see the tides, but this noise I've isolated and consumed tied me here to this city, I couldn't escape.

And even in my dreams, where there is nothing, no noise, the banality of it all creeps in. I open the pantry door. I turn on the kettle to boil. I press the brakes in my car. There is no birdsong in my dreams.

I could devolve to ancestral times. Spend my days singing with the birds, feel my own vibrations and leave language behind. Did you know? We once lived in trees, too.

Dáithí de Buitléir

Ráithín an Chloig, Bré

I bhfad an lae ghairid bhí gor á dhéanamh
ag an drochaimsir; an mhuir, chomh teimhleach
faoin ngruaim le miotal buailte, ag seoladh
rátha muiríní i dtreo an chladaigh.
Tá an dúlra cóirithe i raitín an gheimhridh:
brosna is aiteann. Táim féin théis dreaptha
sa chiúnas arís, thar fhuaim na dtonnta.
Is fada nár chualathas clog nó guí
sa bhallóg seo, béal gan carball;
is an creideamh, ar nós teangan
nach labhraítear le fada an lá – balbh.

Dáithí de Buitléir

Ráithín an Chloig, Bray

Throughout the short day, the bad weather
has been in brood; the sea, as sullen
under the gloom as beaten metal, sending
scallop shoals toward the strand.
Nature is dressed in the cloth of winter:
gorse and bracken. I have climbed
to this silence again, beyond the waves' noise.
It is long since bell or prayer was heard
within this ruin, a mouth without palate;
and Faith, like a language
not spoken in an age – mute.

S.J. Delaney

Queer Pastoral

I sojourn to the country to ride in cars.
City life is tedious. Going to his (buses and taxis)
Or him coming here (tidying and figuring out
How to get rid of him after).
But there? It's pure lovey; fields, dark games
And endless snaking lanes, like the runoff at a beach.
My shopkeep came to meet me, and in the front
Of his car I sucked him off.
In the back of the car he fucked me,
Sitting in the gate of a field, empty and rolled.
When I was a child it was a dump. And now,
Green grass and patches of docks and shamrock
And his BMW hybrid, steaming up.
There's something in those hard finger tips
Like the sleeves of a woollen jumper, pulled over
My shoulders and back. So much tension in his
Worried neck, softened by my maiden's touch,
Softened with the smell of air, petrol, and leather.
We paused only once, to watch headlights pass by,
Though his car, now a rock,
       Sat firm in the landscape; in a field once a dump,
          In a car, in me,
               He shuddered and laughed
          And I walked home in the rain.

S.J. Delaney

I Won't Stop Writing Queer Pastorals

My resistance is being a countryside slut.
Sodomy is a method of spacial reclamation.
I get my PreP in Portlaoise and I take it in
My childhood bedroom. Praxis.

You might look at the rolling plains of the South East,
The Golden Vale and see: an enclosed landscape
Of industrial agriculture, fields of tillage and millions of milking cows,
Deforestation, cut down and shipped off to build British boats,
Land divided and divided as rents hiked higher till BAM. Land acts.
Capitalism. Trending towards monopoly.
Till all there's left is five farms, three closed factories,
Thousands of acres of desperation
                      And one slut.

But me?
I see gaps in the ditch. I see empty sheds.
I see abandoned paths, all calling to be rode in.
Some queers can't move to Dublin,
                Can you imagine?
I think I might feel guilty
                Or unresolved.
The first cock I ever sucked was attached
To a Gemini who then stole my first almost boyfriend.
                            All down by the river.
Where queerness lives, in the dark with the lapping shores
                            And distant foreboding sounds.
I brought another boyfriend down there years later (a mistake).
      One does not visit a battlefield, before the corpses are removed.
It hinders Romanticisation and hurts gentrification.

This was supposed to be an empowering poem.
This was supposed to espouse the poetic beauty
Of the slut life. But it's not to be. Because no matter
How slutty I am there, it's *always there*. Waiting for me.
My hard-fought pride disappears behind grey clouds,
Like a balloon; an unhappy child.
It doesn't sustain us there, I don't think.
There is no empowerment in ditches.
No serving cunt in wandering streams.
No slaying amongst the bewildered heifers.
It drains you, speaking to ghosts.
Among the bails, shadows.
I don't know how to do it anymore.
I don't know how to be without cars,
Cafés, bars, buses, and endless rushing people.
I've been talking for years, spending life trying to find
The queer in the rural, the Queer Eco-Poetics of Kilkenny.
I'm sorry but this might be it,
                Isn't it?

It kinda can't be. The queer pastoral must live.
Some fags can't move to Dublin,
                Can you imagine?
Some gayboys are born on farms.
      Some even wear wellies.
Some queers listen to Lana Del Rey and dream
Of Hollywood, glamour, and see only green green green.

I get my PreP in Portlaoise,
    I fuck in Kilkenny.
        But I'm queer in Dublin.
            And I don't know what to do with that.

Notes on Contributors

Beattie is a writer and lapsed drag queen from Merseyside. Their work has appeared in outlets including *The London Magazine*, *Datableed* and *Briefly Write*. 'Gnomes, Staring up the Hill' was long-listed for the 2022 Spelt Poetry Competition. An extract from their novel-in-progress recently appeared in Writing On the Wall's *Beyond the Storm* anthology. You can follow them on Twitter @poofter_pontiff.

Diarmuid Cawley is from Sligo, Ireland. He lectures on wine, food studies, and gastronomy in TU Dublin. His poems have appeared in *The Martello*, *Trasna*, *Smashing Times*, *Unapologetic Magazine*, *Moonstone Press*, *Guzzle Magazine*, *The Honest Ulsterman*, *Poetry Jukebox* and *Howl: New Irish Writing*. He is working on his first collection.

Scríbhneoir agus file é Dáithí de Buitléir, a bhfuil deich saothar foilsithe aige, cúig úrscéal agus trí cnuasach filíochta ina measc.

S.J. Delaney is a queer Irish writer. His work has previously appeared in *Poetry Ireland Review*, *An Capall Dorcha*, and also *Green Carnations*, an anthology of young queer Irish writing. He has performed at Dublin Pride 2023 and 2022. He is currently looking for a publisher for his first pamphlet. Twitter: @sjdelaneywriter, Instagram: @sjdelaneywriting

Shakeema Edwards is an Antiguan American writer living in Northern Ireland. She recently completed a master's in poetry at Queen's University Belfast.

Chinedu Gospel is a Nigerian poet and an ASSON student from the College of Health Sciences, Okofia. He is also a member of the Frontiers Collective. He tweets @gonspoetry and enjoys playing chess and listening to music when he's not busy with school work or poetry. Some of his works have been published in different online and print magazines and journals. He recently won second place in the Blurred Genre contest,

2023, and an honorable mention in the eighth edition of the Stephen A. Dibiase poetry contest.

Yoni Hammer-Kossoy is a poet, translator, and educator. Winner of the 2020 Andrea Moriah Prize in Poetry, his writing appears in numerous international journals and anthologies. Originally from Brooklyn, New York, Yoni has lived with his family in Jerusalem for the last twenty-five years. Yoni's first poetry collection, *The Book of Noah*, is now available from Grayson Books.

Darren Higgins is a writer and artist living in Waterbury Center, Vermont, USA. His poems, stories, and reviews have appeared in *The Iowa Review*, *Cosmonauts Avenue*, *Jacket2*, *Treehouse*, *Tupelo Quarterly*, *Bloodroot*, *The Rupture*, *Split Rock Review*, *Atlas and Alice*, *Ink & Marrow*, *Poetry International*, and elsewhere.

Ayòdéjì Israel, a poet, writer and editor, holds a Bachelor's degree in English from the University of Ibadan, Ibadan. His work has appeared or is forthcoming in *Eunoia Review*, *Counterclock*, *Defunct Magazine*, *OneArtPoetry*, *Livina Press*, *The Bitchin Kitsch* and elsewhere. You can find him on Twitter @Ayo_einstein.

John Kaufmann is an attorney and mobile home park owner who lives near New York City. His writing has been published in *Off Assignment*, *Ep;phany Online*, *The High Plains Register*, *Tax Notes*, *The Journal of Taxation of Financial Products*, and *The Journal of Taxation of Investments*. Kaufmann blogs at dirtlease.com.

Michael David Jewell lives in Calais, Vermont (U.S.A). Two of his chapbooks were published by Wood Thrush Books, and more recently his poems appeared in *Mizna*, *The Shanghai Literary Review*, *Negative Capability Press*, *Roanoke Review*, and *The Manhattanville Review*. His maternal grandfather was an orphan from County Wexford, indentured in Quebec.

Susanna Lang's chapbook, *Like This*, was released in 2023 (Unsolicited Books), along with her translation of poems by Souad Labbize, *My Soul Has No Corners* (Diálogos Books). Her poems and translations have appeared in *Channel, Prairie Schooner, Asymptote, The Common, Tupelo Quarterly, Circumference*, and *The Slowdown*, among other publications.

Morgan Leathem Ventura is a writer, ex-archaeologist, and translator whose work appears or is forthcoming in *Poetry Ireland Review, The Waxed Lemon, Banshee, Augur, Lackington's*, and *Best Canadian Essays 2021*. Recently shortlisted for the 2023 Listowel Writers' Week Poetry Collection Award, Morgan holds a MA from the Seamus Heaney Centre.

Rose Malone writes short stories and poems in English and has been published in *New Square, The Galway Review, Drawn to the Light Press* and *The Same Page Anthology*. Le déanaí, thosaigh sí dánta a scríobh as Gaeilge freisin.

File dátheangach í Joanne McCarthy agus tá sí ag cur fúithi sna Déise. Tá dánta dá cuid foilsithe i roinnt irisí agus duanairí – ina measc *Aneas, Comhar, Poetry Ireland Review, The Stinging Fly, Rattle, The Honest Ulsterman, An Capall Dorcha, Splonk, The Ireland Chair of Poetry Anthology* and *The Stony Thursday Book*. Is comheagarthóir í ar an iris *The Waxed Lemon*. (@josieannarua).

Podge Meehan is from Limerick but has lived in Cordoba, Spain, for more than a decade. He has an M.A. in Writing from NUI Galway. His writing has most recently appeared in *Channel* (Issue 6), *Moth Magazine, The Cormorant* and *Tolka*.

Thomas Mixon has poems in *miniskirt magazine, Rattle, Radon Journal*, and elsewhere. He's a Pushcart and Best of the Net nominee.

Cliona O'Connell's debut poetry collection was published in 2012. Awards and shortlistings include the Patrick Kavanagh Award, Hennessy Literary Awards, the Trócaire Poetry Ireland Award, the Listowel Single Poem

Award, the Cork Literary Review Manuscript Competition and the O Bhéal International Poetry Competition. Cliona has a Masters in Poetry Studies from Dublin City University.

Is file, scríbhneoir agus craoltóir raidió é Pádraig Ó Cuinneagáin. Roghnaíodh é le beith páirteach i scéim Éigse Éireann Céadlínte in 2022. Go dtí seo tá a shaothar le léamh in *Feasta*, *Howl*, *Comhar* agus ríomhiris Éigse Éireann *Sparks of the Everyday*.

Lani O'Hanlon is a somatic movement therapist and writer living beside the sea in West Waterford. Her writing is published widely and broadcast on RTÉ's *Sunday Miscellany*. Winner of the Poetry Ireland Trócaire Award in 2022, her collection *Landscape of the Body* is published by The Dedalus Press (2023).

Emilia Ong is a British-Chinese Malaysian writer living in the Margate, UK. Scholarship recipient at the Faber Academy, she has published work in *The Guardian*, *Ambit Magazine*, and *HOAX*. In 2021 her current novel-in-progress was shortlisted for the Morley Prize, and in 2022 she was commended for the Laura Kinsella Prize.

Tina Pisco is a West Cork writer of novels, poetry, non-fiction, and short stories. In 2020/21 she became the first Writer-in-Residence for Cork City Libraries, and in 2021/22 was awarded the prestigious Frank O'Connor Fellowship. Her first short story collection (*Sunrise Sunset and other fictions*, FISH 2016) was longlisted for the Edge Hill Prize. Her second collection, *The Dithering: tales from the peri-apocalypse*, has the environmental crisis as an underlying theme.

Hui Ran (卉然, she/her) grows food and attempts to write. Originally from Singapore, she now lives on a homestead in Thailand and enjoys solitude, nature, and the occasional breeze. Instagram: @huiranni

Aoife Riach's poetry has been published in *Poetry Ireland Review*, *crannóg*, *Abridged*, *The Pickled Body* and other magazines. She was a 2019 Irish Writers Centre Young Writer Delegate and was shortlisted for the Marian Keyes Young Writer Award. Her poem 'Vancouver' was selected for the Hungering curation of the Poetry Jukebox.

Born and raised in Belfast, John Tinneny is a writer and translator whose work has appeared in *From Glasgow To Saturn*, *Comhar*, and was longlisted for the National Poetry Competition 2020.

Roman Vai is a writer from Philadelphia. Funk music and peanut butter make him happy. You can read his writing by typing into your search box.

Tremain Xenos lives with his long-suffering wife amid the rice paddies in Japan's smallest and least productive prefecture, where the two raise vegetables and chickens and are currently collaborating on a new novel. Some of his recent stories appear at *carte blanche*, *The Heduan Review* and *Isele Magazine*, among others.

Abby Yucht is an emerging writer living in Jerusalem. By day, Abby works in the field of mental health rehabilitation, and she enjoys running writing workshops for friends and community members by night. Born and raised in Teaneck, NJ, Abby moved to Israel in 2015. Her most recent published works can be found in the literary magazines *Glass Mountain* and *Poetica Magazine*.

Lucy Zhang writes, codes, and watches anime. Her work has appeared in *Apex Magazine*, *Split Lip Magazine*, *CRAFT*, and elsewhere. She is the author of the chapbooks *HOLLOWED* (Thirty West Publishing) and *ABSORPTION* (Harbor Review). Find her at https://lucyzhang.tech or on Twitter @Dango_Ramen.

Thank you to our generous patrons

Hannah Gaden Gilmartin
Sara Nishikawa

We also want to thank those patrons who wish to remain anonymous.